RADIO
IRIS

Anne-Marie Kinney

TWO DOLLAR RADIO
Books too loud to ignore

TWO DOLLAR RADIO is a family-run outfit founded in 2005 with the mission to reaffirm the cultural and artistic spirit of the publishing industry.

We aim to do this by presenting bold works of literary merit, each book, individually and collectively, providing a sonic progression that we believe to be too loud to ignore.

TWO DOLLAR RADIO
Books too loud to ignore

TwoDollarRadio.com
twodollar@TwoDollarRadio.com

For Bill, Mary and Madeleine Jetter

PART I

Quiet

Iris feels goose bumps rising on her forearms, but hesitates to touch the thermostat. Her synthetic leather pumps are filling with sweat, creating an embarrassing squeak when she walks, but those tiny bumps on her arms are rising up in mute defiance. Her ninety-nine-cent eyeliner is melting, a line of chocolate brown stamped now in the creases of both eyelids, but her lips are cold and chapped. Her body cannot agree with itself, and it is two minutes after two o'clock.

When the phone rings, a dull ache passes over her chest as her hand darts out to the receiver. She picks it up in a graceless clatter and coos the corporate-approved greeting, her index finger poised to transfer the caller to his or her desired department. Though her body cannot determine whether the office air is hot or cold, it is definitely dry, and she is fresh out of eye drops. After she has transferred the call to her boss, cloistered in his office twenty feet down the hall, she gets up to stretch her legs. She crosses in front of her desk, which sits next to the front door, a way-station. Facing the door, she bends over, halving and doubling herself at once, pulling her calf muscles tight. Her lank black hair tumbles down to her ankles, hiding her face like a curtain. Behind her, a fluorescent light flickers, casting intermittent shadows onto the closed doors that line the narrow hallway of office suite 2A. She unfolds herself and returns to her chair, where she glances again at the clock on her computer. 2:04.

Suddenly, a door down the hallway opens and the departing sales director emerges carrying a cardboard box filled with framed photos, a small flower vase, and probably more than a few office supplies. As she approaches, a woman of forty with chin-length, prematurely gray hair and a long, slow stride, Iris sits up straighter, unsure of whether she ought to stand.

The woman arrives at the lobby and pauses in front of Iris's desk, the cardboard box perched on her hip like a child. Iris looks up at her expectantly, a woman with whom she has never exchanged more than a few sentences.

"So," the woman sighs.

"Yes?"

"You'll tell him I left?"

Iris nods, maintaining eye contact.

"Thank you." She smiles slightly, inscrutably, then continues out the heavy white door, closing it behind her with a firm click.

Iris stares at the door. From the conference room at the far end of the hallway, the heavy silence is broken by the stalled motor sound of a fax coming in. She closes her eyes and tries to will them to wetness before going to retrieve it.

Storage Room

It is Monday morning, and Iris is compiling her boss's phone messages from over the weekend, the strays left on the central voicemail instead of his personal line. At his request, she has listened to the messages, transcribed them in Arial, his chosen official font, and printed them out. She is stapling the pages when he emerges from his office carrying the telephone from his desk, the cord wrapped tightly around the base. He stops in front of her desk and holds the telephone up delicately, like a server with a tray.

"What," he asks, raising his faint blond eyebrows, "am I supposed to do with this?"

"I'm sorry?"

"It doesn't work. I mean, it works but it doesn't. Tell me, what is a telephone for?" The corners of his thin lips turn up slightly, his response to her response already planned.

"Um, for talking... and listening... to people," Iris tries. It doesn't matter what she says— he'll coax the right answer out of her if she guesses wrong.

He snaps his fingers and points down at her. His tie is off already, an indicator of his stress level. Iris checks his stubble and is relieved to find it under control.

"Precisely. For listening. But I can't listen properly if there's a buzzing in the background, a buzzing that goes away if I shake the cord..." he demonstrates, waving the cord back and forth in a tight motion, "…but then comes right back as soon as I stop, you see?" He drops the cord. "So what am I supposed to do with it?"

"Do you want me to order you a new phone?"

"Yes, of course."

"Okay, I will."

Iris extends her hand with the transcribed messages, thinking the matter solved, but her boss's gaze is focused somewhere on the wall behind her. He still has the phone perched on his right hand.

"Here," she says, "your messages?"

"Right," he says, refocusing on her and taking the pages with his left hand. He sets the phone down a moment to scratch the back of his neck up and down several times.

"I'm not going to throw this away," he continues, "even though it's useless. It's too big. It'll take up my whole wastebasket, I mean. And it might be good for something sometime. I could use the plastic, or the wires. Somebody could. I'm putting it in storage."

With this, he turns and opens the door directly facing Iris's desk, the room inside pitch dark, and sets the phone on the floor just on the other side of the wall. He then shuts it softly, scratches the back of his neck again and ambles back to his office.

Iris looks at the door. The storage room was not always a storage room. It was once an account manager's office, an older, vaguely European man who always dressed in three-piece suits and carried a handkerchief in his breast pocket, a smirking throwback. She never knew where he was from, didn't ask because she enjoyed guessing, though she encountered him rarely, close as he was in proximity.

There were a couple of times, on slow mornings before anyone else had arrived, that he stood by her desk and pontificated while drinking his coffee, each time on the same topic. Were these lectures titled, presented in an auditorium with programs and refreshments afterward, they would be called, You Must Travel, My Dear or How to Be Young.

"How old is it that you are now, my dear?"

"Twenty-four," she would answer.

"Let me tell you one thing. Do not get married. Do not buy a house. It is a waste of your time and of your energy."

"That's two things."

"You should not live in one place. You should wake up and not know what city you are in. Do not spend your money on practical things. Your only expense should be your shoes. Do not have a home, but wear Louboutins, do you see?"

"Okay."

"When I was your age, I was living in Prague. I was an apprentice to a cabinet maker, but I was in the discotheque every night, and by the next summer I was in Madrid."

"Cabinets still?"

"What? No, no, no, you are not taking my meaning," he would sigh. Then he would finish his coffee and go back to his office, returning with a stack of invoices for her to fax out.

But since he left some months ago, his office has become the holding pen for broken appliances, unneeded papers, and surplus office supplies. These are the things that are no longer things, but not yet trash. They are to be forgotten, but reserved. She is not sure whose anxiety is manifested in the storage room, but because she sits across from it every day, she feels that it is her problem to ignore. Iris looks at the door, now kept closed at all times to keep the clutter out of anyone's field of vision. Who knows where all these things were kept before. Opportunity begets utility. The space became, and now it is filling.

She never found out why he left or where he was going. She must have been out sick that day. She must not have been paying attention.

Dream

She is driving through the desert, some desert. There are no other cars on the road, and her destination is clearly ahead, but remote. She does not know when she started driving. She has been driving, always, bent in this same position, and there is no time to stop.

When she finally finds herself at the house, she is surprised. She didn't know this was where she was headed. Her body knew, her hands and feet knew where to turn the steering wheel, where to step on the gas and brake. Only her mind was left out of the process.

But now, here she is. It has been so many years, but it is exactly how they left it. She remembers the horses standing in their corral, the sun reaching through their bodies so they were warm to the touch and gleaming, sweat foaming at the edges of their nylon blindfolds, and the way they stared forward without seeing as she ran her hand down their cheeks. Between the house and the corral, the yard stretched out, its magnitude deceptive. It didn't look like much, but when she was there, there was no place else; there was a feeling of acreage.

Iris parks in the long gravel driveway and gets out of the car. Standing before the house now, she can sense that something is wrong. Time hasn't left the house untouched after all. The paint is cracking, the front door rusted at the edges. The nut trees in front are overgrown, gnarled into and around themselves. How long has it been? The corral is empty, now.

She approaches the door, which she finds unlocked, and enters, calling softly, "Hello? Hello?"

There is no answer. When she turns the corner, into the kitchen, she is startled to see her childhood dog lounging on the breakfast table, his tail lazily brushing the dusty blond wood. Sebastian looks up at her and emits a small whine, and she takes a seat at the table. She looks into his stately German shepherd face and remembers the time she successfully fried an egg on the hood of her father's pickup truck. He wasn't mad. He just scraped it off and told her to feed it to Sebastian on the back porch. He licked up every morsel, and laid his head in her lap in gratitude.

She senses that he will disappear if she touches him. But she can't help it. She leans down and kisses him between the eyes.

Iris wakes up to find that she has fallen asleep with the lights on, fully dressed, and hanging off of the couch. It is as though sleep has hit her with a thunderous slap. She stands up, blinks the spots away, lets the blood run back to her extremities. It's been happening like this. But sudden sleep is better than none at all.

She travels the perimeter of her apartment, flicking off each light, until there is only the moonlight edging in between the curtains. In her bedroom, she takes off her blouse and wool slacks and leaves them where they lie, unhooks her bra, and crawls into bed in only her underwear. As she lies still in her bed, the night breeze jangling a neighbor's wind chimes, she tries to remember the dream. She can feel that there was one. She can feel dusty air lifting off her skin, and the hot white sun, though long gone, is burning somewhere inside her.

Numbers

When she arrives at the office this morning, she finds that there are thirty-three messages in her voicemail box. The first twenty-nine are a misguided fax machine. She sits through each high-pitched squeal until the system gives her the option of erasing it. Three more are from her boss, who has just landed in Europe. The messages are each about five minutes apart. In the first one, he angrily asks where she is. In the second message, he apologizes for the previous message, explaining that he miscalculated the time difference, but to please call him when she gets in. In the third one, he apologizes in advance for his impatience, but explains with increasing ire that he needs her to call him right away. The thirty-third message is another fax machine.

She quickly dials her boss's cell phone. He picks up after two rings, and it sounds as though he is at some kind of sporting event or street riot. He yells into the phone:

"Thank God! Listen, I need you to do me a favor."

"Okay." She has her pen poised over a fresh yellow post-it note.

"Okay."

"Yes?"

"I'm sorry, it's very loud here— I'm in a meeting."

"Okay. What do you need?"

"I need you to call the Spirgarten hotel in Zurich, and ask

them two questions. One: In what room is Mr. Franz Vilmar staying, and Two: what is their fax number."

"Do you need me to fax something to Mr. Vilmar?"

"Yes, obviously. In the file cabinet directly to the left of my desk, you will find a folder marked, Miscellaneous. The piece of paper in the very front of this folder, the first paper you see, needs to be faxed to Mr. Vilmar post-haste."

"Okay, do you have the number for the hotel?"

"I… hold on."

She listens as he yells something unintelligible. There is a crash, and it sounds as though the phone has been dropped. Suddenly, her boss is back on the line, "Hello? Hellohellohello?"

"Yes?"

"Okay, I don't have the number. Just forget it. Or find the number or something. I have to go." He hangs up.

She looks up Spirgarten online, and finds seven hotels in Zurich under some variation of that name. She finds the paper— a list of names she doesn't recognize in two long columns, and starts calling.

It makes her feel momentarily exotic to send faxes and make calls to far-flung locales. She feels privileged to know the appropriate country codes. But she also knows that she's just pressing the same numbers in a different pattern.

Remember

Iris's older brother, Neil, is a traveling salesman. Not door to door. He sells to the people who sell, finds backers, gets products licensed. He has explained it all to her on more than one occasion, but she tends to tune out before he's done. She calls him a traveling salesman, though he has some other, more modern-sounding title, because she thinks it suits his persona. Every time she talks to him, he is in a different city, talking up different wares, be they fist-sized juicers or a wrinkle cream that promises, finally, to stop time. He is always at the airport, in a cab, in a wind tunnel, waiting for the train that's just pulling in. He answers the phone, *Hello? Yeah, I can hear you! What?!*

When he finds himself en route to her city, he sometimes calls to arrange lunch, or dinner, or breakfast if that's all he can squeeze in. He always knows where to go.

I can't believe you've never been, he says. *Elvis fucking Presley used to eat here, I swear to god. You didn't know that?*

He always has an anecdote at the ready, something he read somewhere, though sometimes she can't imagine where, but doesn't press.

This used to be a fabric store, back in the '50s.

Today they are supposed to be having lunch at a Mexican place that was once a speakeasy during the prohibition era.

I hear they still have the tub that was used to distill gin in the back, no joke.

The restaurant is a long narrow hallway. Iris sits waiting at a table against the curved, peach stucco wall, the warmth from the kitchen wafting over her from behind splintered, white saloon doors. A vase in the middle of the table holds two fake daisies, drooping away from each other like a plastic letter *M*. She glances out at the parking lot again. Her phone rings and she looks down at it in her hand for a moment before answering.

"Don't," she says.

"I'm sorry. You know I'm sorry— I couldn't get away."

"How am I to know you're not lying? How would I know if you were just avoiding me, forever?"

"Come on, I said I was sorry."

"Yeah, yeah," Iris sighs.

"Next time, I promise, but I've gotta go now— I have a two o'clock flight and it's... fuck, it's one."

"Yeah," Iris says again, "yeah."

They hang up and Iris orders chicken tacos at the counter. She has lost count of the number of times Neil has stood her up like this. She tries not to think of things she might have done to deserve it, and instead remembers the last time they managed to get together, several months ago, at a Chinese buffet by the airport that he said had served as the backdrop in some old action movie. She'd been in a remembering mood.

"Do you remember when we used to go sledding?" she asked, fiddling with the sticky lid on the soy sauce.

"Used to? When?" he said, sawing at a strip of beef with a plastic knife and fork.

"A bunch of times. You were there. Don't you remember how Sebastian used to sink in the snow? In that weird little parka Mom made for him?"

"When did we ever have snow?"

"We would drive up to the mountains. We would drive around and around until we found a perfect hill, without too many trees or bushes or anything, because Mom was worried we'd impale ourselves." She tried to meet his gaze, but he never looked up from his plate.

"You sure you're not remembering some movie, about some other kids who went sledding? I mean— what mountains, even?" Neil said, then coughed into his napkin and took a sip of soda.

Iris murmured, more to herself than to him, "It was when we lived at that old house, with the horses. There were mountains, not too far anyway…"

Neil gave an exaggerated shrug with his fork in one hand and soda in the other.

"It was so much fun. You had fun…" she started, but lost momentum. She cracked open her fortune cookie, her meal only half eaten. *A man without aim is like a clock without hands, as useless if it turns as if it stands*, the fortune said, and she flicked it onto her plate.

"What are you getting all quiet about?" he continued, wiping a fallen drop of sriracha off his hand with a napkin. "It doesn't make any difference one way or another."

"I just like it when you and I can both remember things."

"I remember plenty of stuff," he said, wiping at a spot on the table now, "try me."

"Never mind," she said, and ate the cookie.

They call her number and Iris goes up to get her tacos, but it's taken so long that her lunch break is over, and she has to take it to go in a Styrofoam box.

As she walks out into the parking lot— five minutes late and counting— she has a sudden memory of playing Go Fish with Neil in their parents' car as it gingerly hugged the mountainside, all their belongings crammed in the trunk and strapped to the roof. All the blankets and pillows were stuffed under their legs, so they were cushioned, their knees up by their chins. The cards were laid on top of a large picture book precariously balanced on the sleeping dog's back. Their parents were listening to Lake Woebegone on tape, an invisible screen between the front and backseats.

"Got any sevens?" her brother asked, absently chewing on his bottom lip.

"Go fish," she replied, though she found the seven of clubs among her cards as soon as she said it. She decided not to correct herself, and stroked the underside of Sebastian's neck with deliberate nonchalance.

Then the car stopped short and cards flew everywhere— on the floor, in their mother's lap, in a firework spray. The book slipped off Sebastian's back as he rose to his haunches, barking angrily, insistently. Iris quickly pulled her hand away from him. Their father put the hazards on while he consulted the map. Iris and her brother turned to look at each other behind the dog's tense, heaving back, all symmetry, as their mother turned around in her seat and softly murmured, "Sebastian, be reasonable," then turned back around, whispering anxiously about something Iris couldn't make out.

As she pulls out of her spot, she imagines Neil driving away, waving back to her through the sunroof, only the tips of his casually flapping fingers visible out the top, like they would be, if he'd shown up. She can always picture him leaving, whether she wants to or not.

Ascent

Neil hangs up, throws the phone back in his briefcase and leans his seat back the inch or two he's allowed. He could have told her earlier that he wasn't going to make it to lunch, that he was going to try to get an earlier flight, but he thought it kinder to appear as though he had tried, had done everything in his power to bend his schedule for her. But the prospect of rushing across town, speeding back to the airport just in time for the sake of another half-hour of high sodium and strained conversation— it was too exhausting, all of it.

He looks out his small window at the tarmac. They've been sitting on the plane now for over forty minutes with no sign of imminent movement— negating the point of the early flight altogether— and he feels pins and needles rushing through every inch of his body, an impotent fury at this halted momentum. His iPod's dead, but even if it weren't, he's sick of everything on it, pressing skip, skip, skip, because the song titles just telegraph the whole song he's heard seven hundred times so he doesn't need to listen to it, so he skips, and skips. There's nothing to read. Before boarding he browsed the newsstand, thought about buying a paper and then didn't. He tried flipping through the airline's magazine, lingering over a top ten list of must-visit burger joints in America, none of which he'd ever been to or probably ever would, but after a few pages, he couldn't shake the feeling that even the articles were ads, even the gloss of the pages against his fingers and the act of turning them was trying to tell him what he should be doing, and what he needed and didn't have.

He realizes he's giving a monologue in his head again and he wants to stop. So he stares out at the black, wet tarmac, and the drizzle dotting the bright yellow windbreaker of a baggage handler as he motors past on a cart leaden with identical black rolling suitcases.

God what a shitty job, he thinks. He turns away from the window and looks around the cabin. Everyone seems to be fidgeting with bags, straps, seatbelts, their hands grasping at things. Even the flight attendants— they're reaching, switching, grabbing. They all know what they're doing, but he can't imagine what all the fussing and mussing is for. It smells like the flu in here, this eighties upholstery, the groaning gray plastic cart stacked with sodas that he can just see parked at the other end of the aisle, sodas that taste like old bubble gum and sit in his stomach like an inflated balloon, and greasy little bags of nuts, and there are thousands upon thousands of them, a constantly replenished supply of bullshit to occupy the hands and jaws, and he'll probably just fucking eat them and drink them because what else is he going to do and then what?

Then they'll finally take off, and after the initial ascent, for those few moments when his ears are popped, and all he hears is the interior of his skull, and his organs feel suspended away from the walls of his body, he'll look out the window at the rushing cloud wall and briefly experience that singular joy of flight, and remember all over again that he, and his body, are alive.

SMOKE

Back at the office, with her boss gone, the day takes on a looseness that Iris doesn't quite know what to do with. Occasionally, she will hear footsteps in the hallway, outside, people passing to and from the restrooms, in and out of offices she has never seen. How do they arrange their furniture? Who sits behind their front desks? She knows there are people in her own office, behind more doors. But she can't say she feels their presence. Every now and then, the phone will ring and she will answer.

"One moment please," she says, and with the press of a button she is alone again.

She listens to several messages accumulated over lunch from people she doesn't know who leave phone numbers but no area codes, or give only first names. Wrongly assumed familiarity is rampant today. Her boss calls at one point and asks her to find a post-it note on his desk with a series of numbers scrawled on it in pencil. *No, not that one. The one next to it. What color is it? No, the green one.* She finds the right one and reads the numbers off to him. He thanks her and hangs up quickly.

She spends the rest of the afternoon going through the files on her computer, making sure they are still organized in a way that she understands. *Click, save, yes, okay.* Then, toward four o'clock, when the air conditioning starts to make her feel rheumy and the recycled air starts to dry out her skin, she becomes suspicious, and then absolutely certain that she smells cigar smoke.

She has always liked the idea of cigars, that warmth of poker games and whiskey, but the smell— it is only good in theory. It is thicker, denser, more pungent than cigarette smoke, but she still feels like a hypocrite, a year-old, half-empty pack of Marlboro Lights in her purse that she dips into every once in a long while.

The stale, musky odor of it is filling the reception area. Her eyes are beginning to water. She leans over her desk and is startled to see the smoke coming in thickly under the door, an amorphous white cloud of it, expanding lugubriously through her space. For a second she feels that something magical must be happening, and she is unprepared for magic. Her throat is burning now and she doesn't know what to do. Soon the smoke alarm will go off, or the sprinklers, they have those right? They must? What does a person do? She searches the ceiling.

And then she becomes aware of music playing, slowly increasing in volume. It starts out as a drum beat, so quiet it might be her heart. It gets ever so slightly louder, louder, until the sound falls into a familiar pattern, the sharply dated sound of a saxophone, and keyboards filling the air with electric dots. She feels a thrumming vibration in her veins. A little louder, and it drowns out her thoughts. She is trapped in the sound now, the smoke still creeping in and she starts to panic. Finally, she gets up from her desk and steps out into the hallway.

The smoke is billowing out from underneath the door of suite 2B, the office that meets 2A at a corner, the restrooms separating them from the suites at the other end of the second floor. There is no sign on the door, no name.

The music grows louder still, the wild festiveness of the saxophone belying the accompanying murk as the smoke forms a hazy wall in front of the door. She steps forward and knocks, her eyes filling with dry, stinging tears.

The music fades slightly, and a crackling, youthful-sounding male voice answers.

"Yeah?"

She clears her throat.

"I'm sorry, but, are you smoking a cigar? Or, uh, cigars?"

After a long pause, the reedy voice behind the door begins to mumble something unintelligible.

"No," he finally says clearly, "it must be somebody else."

"I'm sorry. But… it's just, the smoke looks like it's coming from your office, and it's probably going to set off—"

"Do you want me to turn down the music?"

"No, that's okay, it's just—"

The music abruptly switches over to a somber piano concerto, the volume slowly decreasing until it is barely audible. She stands there for a moment, trying to think of a proper response, and finding none, says thank you, returns to her office and gathers her things. It is a full hour before the usual closing time, but she feels that her excuse is valid. Plus, it's more than likely that no one will ever notice.

In the parking lot, she starts her car and idles in her spot for a moment. A strange giddiness washes over her as she smells the smoke on her clothes, proof that she hasn't imagined any of this. Her phone rings suddenly, pulling her out of the moment. It's Mallory, the screen says, Iris's college roommate. For whatever reason, Mallory continues to seek out her company, whether out of curiosity, pity, or genuine affection Iris is never sure. She decides to answer.

"Hey!" Mallory says, "Are you doing anything tonight? I'm all moved into my new place and it's cute as hell. Come by for drinks?

"Um…"

"Oh shut up, you know you're coming. Nine o'clock?"

"Uh… I…" She can't bear the cigar smell any longer, and rolls down the window. She takes a deep breath. "Okay."

"Perfect," Mallory says, and hangs up.

Iris tosses her phone on the seat. She starts the car and eases out of the spot, the sun hovering above her, contemplating its slow creep downward, as if it has a choice.

Housewarming

When Iris arrives at Mallory's door, she realizes too late that she's been tricked. The music is loud, the kitchen and living room packed with people: a party. Iris drops her jacket on a pile by the front door, folds her arms, and makes her way to the refreshment table, which is appointed with a full bar and a striking array of hors d'oeuvres, from thin baguette slices artfully arranged around a pool of olive oil to a plate of tiny crab cakes speared with toothpicks. The guests are drinking out of glasses— not red plastic cups or chipped mugs, the way parties used to be, senior year, in houses that should have been condemned, scavenged furniture and cigarettes ground out in the kitchen sink.

She pours herself a glass of wine and makes her way through the crowd, avoiding eye contact with the few people she recognizes and the many she doesn't. It's easy to do when everyone is already locked into groups, laughing, chatting madly, spilling drinks and digging around in the kitchen for club soda. The various noises are fighting with each other for her attention.

She steps out the sliding glass door to the balcony where she finds Mallory leaning over the railing, smoking a cigarette. Iris lights up one of her own and leans beside her.

"Why didn't you tell me this was a party? I would've changed clothes, or something."

"No, you would've stayed home." Mallory squints. "But now you're here and it's not so bad, is it?"

Mallory stands up straight now, her green velvet minidress swinging in the breeze. Her dirty blond hair is pulled into a tight ponytail, which she pulls tighter, the end of her cigarette protruding perilously close to the tips of her heavy bangs. Iris does feel underdressed in her wilted work clothes.

"Yeah, I guess, maybe."

Mallory leans in secretively, switching gears without warning. "Did you see a girl holding this cat under her arm like a football."

"A cat? Really? I didn't see that…"

"I like cats as much as anybody, but I don't even know that girl. Who brings a cat to a party? Who even brought her?"

"I think I would have noticed that. Maybe she left."

"Maybe. I've been out here for like twenty minutes."

"Why?" Iris laughs.

Mallory shrugs. "I can't relax anyway. I have to work tomorrow. They sprung it on me yesterday and now I can't have any fun at my own goddamn party."

"You have to work on Saturday?"

"I don't even want to talk about it. They'd go bankrupt without me, I swear."

Mallory turns around to face the sliding glass door and rests her elbows on the railing. She scans the room inside as though appraising the party, calculating the level of fun. Iris looks down at the busy street six floors below. They smoke in silence for a minute, then put out their cigarettes in a ceramic ashtray shaped like a frog. The mouth is filled with sand.

"Oh my God— I almost forgot— there's someone I want you to meet. A friend of mine from work brought him."

Iris leans back on the railing. She rolls further back onto her heels, lets her toes point up at the sky. It occurs to her that she doesn't know how sturdy the railing is. That maybe she shouldn't be dropping her weight. She feels for any sign of give.

"He's really smart, and he's weird. He's old."

"Giving me the hard sell?"

"No, but in a good way. I'm not saying it right. Fuck. I might be a little drunk."

Iris sighs. She sips her wine, licks her teeth. "Which one is he?"

Mallory comes over to where Iris is standing and points.

"I'm probably not going to talk to him."

Mallory rolls her eyes and fiddles with her necklace, the clasp of which has circled round to the front.

"Do what you want. I'm just trying to be a fabulous hostess."

"I can't believe you know this many people."

"I have to go check on the apple turnovers. You coming in?"

"No, I'll see you inside."

Mallory steps through the door and sashays toward the kitchen, clutching and releasing hands as they dart out to greet her.

Iris turns away and looks down at the tops of passing cars, the sounds of various engines blending together with crickets and the languorous wind, creating an endless hum, the vibrating texture of the night. If she closes her eyes, she can separate out each sound, then seamlessly enmesh them again. She drains her glass and turns around, hesitant as she approaches the sliding glass door

Mantra

There are some things that Iris can say that she loves:

She loves to eavesdrop. Whenever she is out in public, she makes an effort to listen to the conversations swirling around her. Most of the time, they are uninteresting, or she cannot gather enough information to figure out what is going on. But every once in a while, she will witness bare, bleeding emotion in the most inappropriate places. Her all time favorite was the time she heard a woman in a convenience store cry hoarsely into a cell phone, "You never loved me. You tried damned hard but you never did." Her face was red and blotchy, and several strands of hair fell sloppily out of her loose ponytail as she ran her index finger over a can of tomato soup again, and again and again. Iris hated herself for the thrill this moment gave her, but there was pleasure in the guilt. She imagines that this is similar to what a masochist must feel as a needle pierces the soft skin underneath a fingernail. If someone were to tap her on the shoulder at one of these moments and ask her what she was doing, she would not have an answer.

She loves to look at a photograph of Neil, at maybe nine or ten years old, holding their dog, Sebastian, on his lap. The dog is enormous on his small, knotty, bare legs. He peeks out from behind Sebastian's long upright trunk with a goofy, unselfconscious grin, squinting against the sunlight. She keeps this photograph on the green wooden desk in her bedroom, underneath what she privately calls The Pile of Importance— mostly insurance papers, pay stubs, and other bits of paper that they say a person is supposed to keep. When she looks at this photo, she feels the heat of so many summertime backyards, of the satisfaction of putting foxtails in her hair in a neat row, her father snapping picture after picture of the clouds moving overhead, while her mother sipped iced tea, and crunched down on the ice cubes. The photo is a close-up, so there's no telling where it was taken, which house, which summer. But Neil is young enough in it, that she can place it vaguely, in an era. She tucks it away again. It is the only photo she has.

When she is driving, stuck in traffic or spacing out at a red light, on her way to or from work, sitting still, lazy fingers hanging off the bottom of the steering wheel, Iris often repeats these images in her mind, over and over, like some kind of visual mantra. She knows she is doing it again when cars behind her start honking. She doesn't know why. She can't stop.

When she snaps back into reality, she turns up the radio. She knows every song in rotation at the local oldies station, and hums along, quietly, in the back of her throat.

She loves music more than anything else on earth, and without it, she is certain that she would die.

LUNCHTIME

At twelve-fifteen, Iris leaves the office as she does most days— locking the door and setting the elaborate alarm system if she is alone or the last to leave— and walks three blocks to a café. She orders a chicken sandwich with a side salad, takes her food out onto the patio, and sits down facing the side-walk. Sometimes, she reads thrillers from the seventies with titles like *Blood Secrets*. Other times, she reads fashion magazines. But mostly, she listens to the two old men at the next table. They sit huddled, as co-conspirators, trading information over egg salad. They wear suits and hats on even the hottest days. They always seem agitated, shaking their heads at the ground. Iris listens to them talk about their daughters— the bums they're dating, the cars they neglect. They talk about tomatoes that won't grow and new neighbors they can't seem to warm up to. They go through cup after tiny cup of espresso. But their most common topic is their declining health.

"Every morning I wake up," the taller one says, "and my legs feel like they're filled with fishing weights from ankle to thigh, pulling me to the ground."

"I wake up every morning," the other one says, "and I can't even feel my legs, so count yourself lucky."

"I don't know which is worse."

"Me either." The two chuckle breathily then, and the tall one takes his hat off and sets it on the table.

She has been reading the same magazine for a month, holding her place half-heartedly, with a finger. She listens, staring at the white space on the page.

She returns from lunch, and walks down the lavender carpeted hallway, unusually gloomy due to a burnt-out light bulb. She stops when she sees that the door to suite 2B is wide open. No one in the building leaves their doors open. They don't want business to mix; it's unseemly. In fact, she knows what other businesses reside in the building only by the names on the doors and sheer guesswork. Delaney & Schmidt: Law firm, personal injury. Meridian Corp.: Consulting. Maybe image consulting. She could have it all wrong.

And her own door, Larmax, Inc. She hasn't figured out yet what that sounds like. She's heard her boss refer to himself countless times as a businessman, in the business of moving money. She's typed out letter after letter referring to various deals and agreements, sums and figures with no apparent context, but they never get more specific than that. She wonders if he or any of his past or present associates could explain precisely what it is they do, if she asked, or would they just laugh and ask her to get them some coffee?

The door of 2B is open, and as far as she can see, it is only one small room. She sees a desk, a chair, a computer. Nothing seems out of the ordinary, until she notices the full-size refrigerator, kitchen sink and counter strewn with piles of dirty dishes, filling up a full quarter of the room.

She gets to her own door and struggles with the lock. Her key is a copy of a copy of a copy, so it is barely a key at all, more like a key-shaped nub, and brute force is required to make it work. She turns, pushes, pulls, and still the door won't budge. She pulls the key out and massages her temple. *This is how I get fired*, she thinks. *They change the locks.*

She glances back at the open door, so close to her own they are practically kissing, a wall shared between the two offices. She cranes her neck to see if she can see anything else, and then she takes a step. One more step and she's inside.

On one wall, a yellowing map of the United States is tacked up with push pins. Against the opposite wall sits a massive wing chair of deep green velour and a small side table topped with a lamp made from or made to resemble a horse's hoof. She touches the coarse hair and flinches, certain that it is real. The office is barely the size of a studio apartment— not even. There is not even a place to put a bed. There is a vague smell of smoke, tempered some by the open window. There are no blinds, so the sun shines a blinding spotlight into the room.

Iris steps closer to the chair and reaches out to touch it, her hand brushing back the soft green fibers. She closes her eyes.

Then a muffled clang from the doorway cuts through the moment, and her arm shoots back to her side. She turns around slowly to find a young man, skinny, in jeans and a stained white T-shirt, a cardboard box dropped at his feet.

"Oh," she murmurs.

He doesn't say anything, and she looks not at him, but around him, at the edges of him. She remembers a middle school teacher who instructed her to look at her classmates' foreheads if she got nervous while giving an oral report. She aims a little higher, a little off to one side. She is standing right in the sun's spotlight and wants desperately to get out of it, so she makes her move, approaching the doorway quietly, her gaze still unfocused, taking nothing in. She edges past him awkwardly, his body monolithic in its stillness, and out into the hallway. She grabs for her door-knob, finding the office unlocked now. Someone has beaten her back from lunch while she stood spellbound in the other room. She sucks up the cool air and rests against the door, hears the other door slam shut. She would regret her boldness, and maybe it was misplaced, but she doesn't want to regret. What she wants is to go back, to knock and be let in. To sit in the soft green chair and sink into a deep and dreamless sleep.

Going Out

Under duress, Iris has agreed to go out with Shawn, the man from the party, but she doesn't know what Mallory was thinking. He is tall, appealingly rangy in a way, his brown hair a little overgrown, and he is dressed in that studied casual way of most older men— the ones she has met, anyway— a black T-shirt, charcoal gray suit jacket, and pressed jeans. He is also thirty-eight and a father of two, a fact she didn't learn until tonight.

He is walking her home from a dark but relatively quiet bar just around the corner from her apartment, where she had two white chocolate martinis. She is not drunk, but she could be. As he asks her questions about herself, she half listens and half flips a switch in her mind, drunk/not drunk. She could argue either position. But it's easier to blame it on drunkenness, this restless contrarian streak she feels taking hold.

"So, which do you prefer," he asks, hands in his pockets, his jeans draping just so, "the city or the country?"

"I don't know… neither?"

"Come on, you've got to pick one."

"Water, then."

"You mean, like the beach?"

"No, I… never mind."

"No, what do you mean?"

"I thought I was telling a joke."

"Oh. Okay, I think I get it."

They walk in silence for a minute as a wailing ambulance passes, its siren fading in the distance just as quickly as it appeared.

"So," he starts in again, "you never told me what you studied in college."

"I didn't go to college."

"But, I thought you and Mallory were roommates?"

"Oh, I went. But it may as well have never happened. I remember almost nothing about it."

"Yeah," he says, "the past does have a way of disappearing on us. I never took pictures before the kids came along, then I had to. They changed every time I looked at them."

He smiles at her, but she is watching their feet on the pavement, following the disjointed rhythm of their steps side by side. She stops walking and looks up at him as he stops too.

"That's the most terrifying thing I've ever heard."

They arrive at her doorstep and she digs around in her purse for her keys. She finds them and gets the door open, then turns back to face him.

"Thank you," she says.

He leans in to kiss her cheek, but she is caught off guard and swivels her head away, and his lips land in her hair. She exhales another thank you and rushes inside. She doesn't look back.

THE LONG NIGHT

On this night, she fills the tub with hot water and lavender-scented oil that makes her skin feel like shiny fabric. She moves the radio into the bathroom and listens to the oldies station. It is request and dedication hour. She soaks, staring at the ceiling and listens as a man dedicates "Unchained Melody" to his fiancée:

"This is for you, Steph, because you'll always be my baby."

The familiar notes kick in and she vows once again that she will never love a man who would consider dedicating this song to her on the radio. Other songs included in this pledge are "When a Man Loves a Woman," and "Let's Get It On." Not that this is a relevant concern at present, but she likes to remind herself that she has standards. She lowers her head into the water and lifts the drain plug with her big toe. Her body emerges as the water disappears down the drain, and she lies in the cold, empty tub for a few minutes. A woman calls in to request "Not Fade Away" by Buddy Holly and she closes her eyes, imagining this woman dancing in a plush carpeted living room with yellow walls, an army of small children dancing around her in a circle.

The bath was an attempt to lull herself gently to sleep and, like every other method she has tried, it has failed. She tried drinking warm milk before bed, but was unable to get past her conviction that warm milk, at its core, is revolting. She considered running to wear herself out, but abandoned that when it became clear, once she was standing in her living room dressed in jogging gear, that this would require her to run.

As she lies awake on this night, she begins to resign herself to the fact that sleep will only come to her suddenly or not at all, and this will most likely be a not-at-all night. First, there will be two to three hours of non-specific, low-grade panic. She will lie still and worry about everything from the depletion of the world's natural resources to the fact that she cannot remember when she was last at the dentist. She will then fall into a sleep-like trance for an indeterminate amount of time, during which she will have dream-like visions. A recent vision had her sitting in a diner, resting her head on the lunch counter. She was about to fall asleep when the cook pulled a large tray out of the industrial-sized oven and placed it directly in front of her. She slowly lifted her head, and looked down to find a tray of warm sleeping animals. She picked up a squirrel and held its small face against hers.

At some point in the still-dark early morning, she will look at her digital alarm clock, but she will not note the time. She will then mentally walk herself through the coming day, from what she will wear to who will call the office and what she will say to them. Then her alarm will go off, and the day will begin just as she has planned.

Broken

When things in the office are broken, no one knows what to do. Or, no one quite does anything. When the printer is low on ink, everyone learns to accept the blank strip in the middle of the page. Everyone would rather pretend they can read the faded letters than go dig a new cartridge out of the supply closet. *Just pull it out and shake it*, someone will say, *that'll hold it for a while.* Today, it's the coffeemaker that's broken. Someone must have put in a fresh filter, filled it with Colombian roast, pressed the red button, and walked away or gotten distracted, never to discover that the machine was possessed. That's what must have happened, Iris assumes, when she walks into the break room and finds the counter drenched in proto-coffee and un-brewed crystals, the machine still spewing viscous brown sludge until she unplugs it. She lays paper towels out across the counter and watches them soak up the liquid instantly, until they are maxed out, floating above the still-wetness. She slides these into the trash and lays out another layer, then another, until the counter is dry, then runs a wet cloth over the surface, sinking her nails into the cool folds of cotton. As she is doing this, her boss walks in, returned from his travels, and for a moment she is sixteen again, working behind the counter at the Donut King and he is a customer, jangling the bells on the door with his arrival and surveying the offerings, wide eyed. She sets the rag down and looks askance.

"Is there coffee?"

"No."

"Why not?"

"It's not working." She shrugs in the direction of the coffeemaker.

"Did you try hitting it?"

He steps in front of her and gives the machine an open-palmed slap. The plastic hinge of the lid comes loose with a pop.

He sends her to the café with a five dollar bill and a list of three desirable espresso drinks, of which she is to choose one. He says he feels like being surprised, but not too surprised. She is happy to be sent outside. She steps out of the building and onto the sidewalk, the breeze blowing her hair into her face. She clutches the money in her fist and squints against the sun, smoothes her hair back. It flies forward again.

This neighborhood is hers and not hers. She comes here five days a week, drives here, knows where to find the nearest dry cleaners, record store, place to buy gum. But she is a visitor, still. She has never walked these streets in flip flops, or passed an afternoon wandering through these shops. And if she didn't work here, she would never see these streets again. There just wouldn't be any reason.

She orders him a large hazelnut latte and waits for it, perusing the stacks of weeklies by the door. One cover promises a definitive list of the 100 best pop records of all time, but she can't bring herself to pick it up.

Out of the corner of her eye, she watches as a man and woman stare at each other across a table. She thinks she detects traces of contempt in their stares, in the hard silence between them, but their demeanors could be warped by the nature of her peripheral gaze. The barista sets the cup up on the counter and Iris grabs it.

As she is pushing open the swinging glass door, she hears the man say softly to the woman, "Calm down."

When she returns, her boss is sitting at her desk, squinting intently at her computer screen. She puts his coffee and change down in front of him and stares, deliberately letting the change clatter against the desktop. She fiddles with her fingernails and waits until it seems he will never notice her. She considers laying her palms on the desk and staring him down, but she doesn't. He could look up at any moment.

"Sir?" she finally says.

He blinks as though waking from a hypnotic state and looks up at her.

"Oh, oh," he says, noticing the coffee cup, "Great, great— I'll be done here in one second. My computer's acting screwy again and I had to check something."

He clicks the mouse and gets up from her chair, awkwardly extricating himself from the tight space between desk and wall. She stands aside as he gathers the pile of coins and drops them in his pocket. He takes a gulp of coffee and winces.

"Jesus Christ— why does it have to be so damned hot?" He sticks his tongue out as though air will ease the burn. Iris notices the dryness of his mouth, the wind-burned rawness of his lips.

"Tell me about it," she says, and then wonders why she said it.

He turns, still grimacing, and hurries off in the direction of his office.

She sits down, sets down her purse, and checks the inbox at the edge of her desk. At the top of the stack, she finds a letter in her boss's handwriting, written on blue-lined notebook paper, with a post-it note stuck on it: Please type and mail thanks! She opens a fresh document on her computer and sets to typing, struggling to interpret certain words in his uniquely tight and sharply angled lettering:

Dear Mr. Leonard,

I enjoyed speaking to you on the phone last week, and am very interested in pursuing the project we discussed. We are prepared to propose a liberal budget for phase one– to say the least– if you wish to do business with us.

However, I was frankly surprised to learn that you have also been in talks with Dimwell, Inc. I understand that you wish to "keep your options open" as it were, but in order for us to feel secure in proposing the figure we are prepared to propose, we need you to make up your mind.

In closing, what's it going to be, Mr. Leonard? Us or them? I await your response with bated breath.

Sincerely,

Your partner??

She reads this through only after she has finished typing it, and wonders whether this is all meant to go in the letter, or whether her boss was venting for his own benefit. She doesn't know if this is the way business is done, has nothing to compare it to, so she is in no position to ask if he really wants this sent. Of course he does. The note said so. She prints it on company letterhead and stamps it with his signature, a stamp he had made after he calculated the amount of time he had spent signing things in his life. At least three years and one month, he said, though she doesn't know how he came up with that figure. She finds the address in the contacts database, prints it on an envelope, affixes it with a forty-four cent American flag stamp, folds the letter inside, and slides it into the outgoing mail tray on the wall by the door. Later today, the mailwoman will place the letter in her satchel with all the others, carry it around with her for the rest of her route before dropping it at the post office where it will spend a few mysterious days in the system, being carted from one place to another before winding up on a plane, then a truck, in a box, in a bag, before it arrives, perhaps a little weathered, on Mr. Leonard's desk. She tries to imagine all the movements and actions necessary to transport this letter across state lines, the hands of each person who will touch it. She sees the placement of their calluses, the rings on their fingers, hangnails or none, nails chewed or painted. Then the phone rings, and it all vanishes.

DESCENT

At the end of the day, Iris switches off her computer, arranges her desk so everything is parallel, stapler, scotch tape, telephone. She sets the code on the phone so that when people call, her recorded voice will say, *Thank you for calling Larmax, Inc. If you know your party's extension, please enter it now. Otherwise, please leave a message. Thank you.* She thinks the second thank you sounds abrupt and redundant, but there didn't seem to be any other way to end it. The idea of saying goodbye on a recording unnerved her for some reason, like she would be turning herself into a ghost.

She stands up from her desk and looks down the empty hallway. Her boss has been closed up in his office all afternoon. The others, she hasn't seen.

"Good night," she calls out quietly, and makes her way out the door.

Walking toward the staircase, she hears a door open and shut, then footsteps on the carpet, catching up to her own. She doesn't look back, and she doesn't look up as she feels this person's presence beside her, and they both turn down the stairs.

They are walking side by side now, and she lets her gaze slide upward, just for a second, to confirm her inkling that it is the man from 2B. He seems shorter walking beside her like this, closer to her own height. He looks a little feverish, his dark hair greasy, but she is stirred by his scent, like dirt, like he has been digging, has only just climbed out of the earth. He stares out into the middle distance, though there is none. There is only the wall ahead. She quickly shifts her gaze to her opposite side, to another wall, the painted and re-painted banister, the very edge of the carpet where no vacuum cleaner can reach, a gray line holding the stairs in, insulating the building in whispers of dust that pile up and will continue to pile. *There could be an echo here*, she thinks. *If I said something, it might echo back.*

They turn in unison at the landing and continue down the second flight, Iris watching the stairs ahead of her now, and the pointed toes of her shoes as they cross each one, down and down. All she hears is the rustle of his jeans.

They reach the bottom of the stairs and Iris darts in front, beating him to the back door. She swings it wide open and he follows, their paths splitting as she approaches her car and he his, on the other side of the lot. She gets into her car and watches out the window as he opens the back of a hulking white van with tinted windows, pulls out a cardboard box, over which he drapes a dirty down comforter, and carries it back into the building. She starts the car and pulls out of the lot.

Iris understands that there are times when she physically cannot speak, when her vocal chords and her mouth can't make a connection. But what is it that she would say, if she could? Even the voice in her head seems to leave her at these times, and then what? It is as though her essence, the *her* in her is rattling around aimlessly, so small, lost in the winding corridors of her body. She drives toward home, the sky fading pink, and she grips the steering wheel a little tighter. She turns on the radio and "Incense and Peppermints" is playing. She turns it up, and the sun keeps sinking. Her pulse feels quick, like she has had too much coffee, though she's had none. She feels that if she let it, her heart could push its way out of her chest, her blouse flapping with its beat, blood soaking through in an ever expanding circle.

Waiting at a red light, she wonders if it would be so strange if she went back to the office. She imagines the man, holed up in his suite, alone in the building by now. What could he be doing? What would he do if she knocked on the door, or didn't knock— what if she just walked in and sat down cross-legged on the carpet, if she looked up at him expectantly, expecting what?

Turning onto her street, Iris imagines a host of scenarios. He doesn't notice her. She kneels beside him as he works on whatever he is working on and he never looks up, even as she breathes heavily, an inch from his forearm. Or— he looks to her. He says, *please stay.* He says, *I was wondering when you would come back,* or *I need to tell you something,* or *sit down,* or *close the door behind you,* or *I've been waiting,* or *you don't know how alone I am*— or *hello. Hello.* That would come first, wouldn't it? And anything at all could come next. She pulls into her parking spot and turns off the car, closing her eyes and focusing on the tinny, coughing little noises of her engine settling into repose. She leans back in her seat for a moment. In the reverberating quiet of the garage, if she listens closely, she can hear the coursing of her blood.

SHOEBOX

Neil wakes up as the plane makes a bumpy landing. In the dream that was just beginning to fade, he had found his parents living in a shoebox under his bed. Kneeling down to face them, he hadn't asked them why they were living in a shoebox, but rather, how they had landed where they did.

He ponders this as he makes his way through the terminal, past the pizza kiosks and keychain booths, the banks of TV monitors and payphones. He hasn't spoken to his parents in some time, not due to any kind of ill will, really. Chatting on the phone just doesn't seem to fit into the rhythm of his days, theirs either, he imagines. They've just moved again, Iris mentioned to him. He figures he ought to get their new address some time, before they move again.

In the dream, he took to carrying the shoebox around with him, because he didn't know what else to do. He'd be driving, and would glance over at them on the passenger seat, his mother feeding the dog, his father cooking breakfast, all their belongings in miniature, neatly arranged against the walls of the little box. His car began to fill with the smell of bacon.

At a red light, he finally asked them if they needed him to take them anywhere, while he was out. He said he had a lot of work to do, and maybe they had someplace they'd rather be.

"Oh, don't mind us, honey," his mother said, her neck severely craned to look him in the eye. "We're fine. Just do whatever you're doing, and we'll do the same."

And he didn't have anything to say to that.

HELLO?

Following a morning spent shredding great stacks of papers— a supply continually refreshed by her boss, tiptoeing behind her to slide another pile behind her ankles and skulking off as she turned around— Iris returns from lunch to find a pile of dollar bills sitting on top of a note on her desk, a sheet of notebook paper with the words *Please get rubber bands* written on it in blue ballpoint ink. She can hear her boss talking loudly in his office, either on a phone call or rehearsing for one. Okay, she thinks, picturing herself slinking onto the front porches of thirty or forty strangers' homes to steal the rubber bands off of their afternoon newspapers, slyly pocketing the cash. No problem. Maybe she will wrap them all together into a rubber band ball, like Neil did endlessly in fifth grade, his bedroom floor littered with multicolored globes of varying sizes, slapstick lying in wait. How convenient it would be to have them all together like that. But how would she start it? How would she fashion the core? She doesn't remember that part. She turns around and back out the door, purse still tucked under her arm.

She walks the three blocks to the drugstore slowly, wishing to prolong the errand, to enjoy her solitude and the sounds of the street. The cars rush by, speeding through crosswalks with no lights, never hesitating, and the wind causes her hair to fly messily behind her like a mass of weeds.

She stops when she sees a shoddily mounted chain link fence

around a vacant lot, just half a block down from the office. It seems to her that there used to be something there, but she can't say what it was. She feels that she would remember a vacant lot, would probably stare at it on a semi-regular basis. There is a rusted metal sign on a post, jammed into the patchy grass just on the other side of the fence. On bumper stickers affixed to the sign, in big block letters, it says:

I'm home.

I'm home.

I'm home.

There, in three rows, like a chant. She stands staring at the sign for a moment. She wonders who put the stickers there. What were they trying to say, or cover up? Is there something underneath the words, or was this a blank sign, erected in service of the people, to display the message of their choosing, first come, first serve?

As she walks on, she keeps hearing the words repeated in her head, in some voice other than her own, *I'm home.* It is neither a woman's voice, nor a man's, and the longer it keeps repeating, *I'm home, I'm home, I'm home,* the more disquieting it is, this voice inside of her that she has never encountered before. She walks faster in an effort to overtake it, to leave it behind her in the crosswalk.

She buys a large bag of rubber bands at the store, and when the cashier hands her the change, her eyes wander to a display of Sharpies at the register. She blinks, and picks up a black one. She weighs it in her palm and folds her fingers around it.

"How much?"

On Iris's way back to the office, a woman, half a block ahead of her, steps into the crosswalk, little yellow lights flashing on the pavement to indicate her right-of-way, and a mere second later, a silver SUV comes barreling toward the intersection, with no sign of slowing. Iris sees it at the same moment the woman does. She stops and watches as the woman first waves an arm, thinking the car needs only a stronger indication of her presence, before, in a panic, she changes tactics, jumping back to the sidewalk a second before the car blows through the intersection. The woman turns around and watches it go, and what Iris sees on her face isn't indignation, or even fear, but pure speechless puzzlement, as though her understanding of things has just floated up and away like a white balloon.

Iris continues walking, and as she approaches the woman, who is still standing motionless on the corner, she wants to say something to her, to let her know somehow that someone has seen.

When she is close enough, she blurts out, "I know," but she doesn't think the woman hears it. She turns back a few seconds later, and the woman is walking, quickly, away. Iris quickens her own pace to match.

She stops again in front of the vacant lot.

I'm home.

I'm home.

I'm home.

She is just barely able to squeeze her arm through and reach the sign, uncapped marker in hand.

On the first line, she writes: *Are you?*

On the second line: *Where?*

On the third line: *So what?*

She has a little more trouble freeing her arm from the fence, and is left with a long white scratch from wrist to elbow. She licks her index finger and rubs it on the scratch, rendering it almost invisible.

When she gets back, the office is locked. She finds her key, and struggles for the thousandth time with the lock while vaguely watching 2B. She tries to switch to her peripheral vision, blur the part of her gaze that sees the doorknob in front of her, her own hand grasping it, and focus on the side view, the other door, freshly painted and serenely closed, quiet emanating from its borders. *He's not in there*, she thinks, *nobody's in there*. This trick works for a couple of seconds, but a twinge of pain in her left eye socket shifts everything back into place as her own door finally comes unlocked. She pushes through and the alarm sounds. Perplexed, she disengages it. She checks the clock on her cell phone. It is not even two o'clock. She was gone for twenty minutes tops.

She knocks on her boss's door and there is no answer. He must have had an off-site meeting he didn't mention to her. Or he felt ill, got a headache. There are countless reasons to leave a place.

She sits at her desk and takes the phone off of automatic answer. Just then the phone rings.

"Thank you for calling Larmax, Inc. How may I help you?"

"Hello," a man says, "I'd like to speak to the owner, please."

"He's not in at the moment. Would you like to leave a message?"

"No, that's all right. Perhaps someone on your sales team might be able to help me?"

"Certainly. I'll see if someone's available. One moment, please."

She dials four for sales and the phone rings until a recording comes on to tell her that the person she has dialed is not available. She dials five, the other sales extension. This time there is no ring at all. She transfers back to the main line.

"Hello, sir?"

"Hello?" she repeats.

He's gone. The sound on the other end is a quiet hiss, so light it disappears when she stops concentrating on it. Iris hangs up.

She sits for a moment with her hand still on the receiver. Then she stands up and heads toward the hallway. She knows her boss is out, or he has chosen to be unreachable, barricaded behind the door. She swivels around to the door that faces his, the accountant's office. She knocks. When there is no answer, she knocks again. Finally, she opens the door to find the office empty, though the computer is on, the plant on the windowsill seemingly in good condition. She approaches it to see if it's real, running a hand delicately over the surface of a leaf, before unintentionally contracting her fingers so the leaf crumbles, staining her fingers a sticky green.

She knocks on each of the junior sales team's doors, and finds that they too are currently empty, though projects sit mid-completion on every desk, files and drawers open. She has a brief inclination to check seats for warmth, but decides this would look bad if someone were to walk in. She skips the sales director's office, knowing it to be empty, but then she wonders, is anyone going to take over for her? It's been a couple of weeks since she left, and two more weeks since she gave notice. As far as she knows, no one has been interviewed, nor anyone promoted from inside.

She checks the rooms one by one and finds them each uninhabited. There are photos on desks. Papers and pens left out. A cold, half-full coffee mug at the edge of one desk, which she picks up, uncovering a dark brown ring.

She shuts the door to each office after she has checked it, and when she is done, she stands in the middle of the hallway. If someone were watching, they would see the expression frozen on her face, eyes narrowed and mouth slightly open. She stands still as a deer hearing footsteps. She stands, feet in an unconscious third position, her body's memory of the childhood ballet classes she has long since forgotten. Her arms hang at her sides.

So, she thinks. *So.*

Finally, she returns to her desk and sits. There is a lot of day left, and her boss will most likely be back. Anyone could be back at any moment. Her breath is shallow. If someone were listening, they would hear just how quiet Iris can be while still occupying space.

She doesn't have any particular task to attend to, nothing in her inbox. She pulls the Sharpie out of her purse. She then takes a sheet of labels out of her desk's top drawer, and writes on one of them, *Property of Iris Finch*.

She peels off the label and sticks it on the marker, smoothing it slowly to prevent wrinkles. She blows on the fresh ink, then sets the marker on her desk, in line with everything else. She leans back in her chair and it rolls slightly forward, creaking. She thinks of putting her feet up on the desk, but she doesn't have enough room, her desk as close to the wall as they could get it and still fit a person in between. She leans back a little further and her head touches the wall, her hair smooth against dried paint. She gazes up at the ceiling, but there's nothing to see there. She thinks back to a time in college when she and Mallory each took a box of Dramamine. At the end of the night, she lay alone on her bed, watching as words passed by in shadow on the ceiling, too quickly for her to read, until they weren't even in English anymore, but some kind of Arabic script. Then she stopped trying to read it, and simply enjoyed the shapes as they flitted past. When she woke up the next morning, she felt a certain sadness that words would most likely never appear to her again as they had that night. She looked up at the flat white ceiling, strangely bereft.

But, she told herself then, *you never know. At least there's that.*

PRIVATE GRAFFITI

Iris begins by labeling her belongings. On the underside of her couch, she affixes a label which says, *If found, please return to Iris Finch.* She adds another: *If found, she probably has bigger problems than the couch.*

She puts a label inside her pillow case which says, *This will last only until laundry day.*

On the bottom of the left shoe of her least favorite pair, it now reads, *My associate and I are bound to die never truly having lived,* in miniscule lettering.

At the office, she keeps things simple, labeling her stapler, notepad, and white-out with only her name.

When she finds that she has run out of blank labels, she takes to writing directly onto things.

On the wall behind the water cooler, in very small letters, she writes, *I will never be thirsty.*

Underneath her phone, she writes, *Stop calling.*

On the underside of her desk, she writes, *Hello and good luck with the earthquake.*

When her boss is out of town again, he calls her one day with instructions to pry open a loose floorboard behind his desk.

"I'm sorry?" she replies.

"Just trust me. It's already loose, no grunt work involved."

"What about the carpet?"

"That's not an issue."

"Okay… and then what?"

"There's an envelope underneath the floor, okay?"

"Uh-huh…"

"A sealed envelope. I need you to overnight it to my hotel."

"Um…"

"No, it's easy. You can pry it open with a spoon, or a pen even, I mean, maybe."

"Okay." Iris scans her desk for an appropriate tool.

"I'm at the Hyatt, okay? Room 312? Will you do that, please?"

"Yes. You'll get it."

"Perfect. I've got to go now."

Iris hangs up and decides to try using a pen, but when she goes to his office and looks behind the desk, she sees that there is a faint rectangle in the carpet. She easily peels it up, and the floorboard is so loose, in fact, that she lifts it with her fingers. She finds the dusty manila envelope, brushes it off, and replaces the floorboard and carpet flap.

Before she leaves his office, she removes a post-it note from a pad on his desk and writes, *What am I up to?* She folds the note until it is the size of a fingernail, then tucks it into the back of his desk's top drawer.

At lunch that same day, she sits near the two old men. They are deeply involved in a game of chess. She watches them with a sideways glance, still ostensibly facing down at her magazine. They say nothing, communicating in concentrated stares at the board, followed by boastful glances at each other, squinting eyes and smirks. The only table she could get is right in the sun, and she feels it burning her arms. She tries to fold herself inward, to minimize her surface, and eats her sandwich with her elbows practically in her lap. The men are safe in the shadow of the café's green-and-white striped awning, and the cover of their jackets. They are in a separate climate from her, Iris thinks. They are so far away over there that the weather is different.

When the game is done, they shake hands and the taller one

begins packing up the board and tucking it into a worn, brown leather case. Once they are gone, she, finished eating, stands and weaves her way over to their vacated spot. On a napkin, she writes, *Teach me to play*, and tucks it under the metal base of the table.

On a Thursday Night

Iris lies in bed, on her side, rose quilt covering her head so she is enveloped in a hothouse of her own breath, with the foggy moonlight arcing through the open window. Slowly, her weight shifts, slowly, slowly, until she is facedown and her head begins to slip, inch by inch, down the edge of the bed, taking the covers with her like a human landslide, her momentum building.

But she hasn't fallen yet. She is having the dream again.

She's sitting at the kitchen table, and it is bright outside, but musty inside the old house. There is nobody there. She has been sitting at the table a long time, legs crossed so they have lost all feeling. She feels immobile, leaden. Finally, like tearing off a band-aid, she uncrosses her legs and massages them from ankle to thigh, gasping as the pins and needles set in.

When equilibrium has returned to her limbs, she rises and walks to the counter, where she finds a carton of milk next to the sink. All the windows are shut, so the silence has nowhere to travel. The silence stays put. She picks up the carton and it is lukewarm, nearly full. She opens the fridge, empty, and sets it on the middle shelf.

She steps out of the kitchen, leaving her shoes at the edge where tile meets carpet, and goes down the dark hallway toward the other end of the house. She opens the back door and steps out into the giant backyard with its single fig tree looming in the distance, letting the wind set the screen door flapping behind her. She steps into the dry grass, and the blades prick the soles of her feet. The sun is on its way down, sitting now at eye level, a radioactive white scrawl across the landscape. The wind rolls, howling its song into her hair and through her clothes. She approaches the fig tree, grass crackling under each footstep, and suddenly, birds erupt from its branches in a great flapping horde. In shadow like this, they could be bats. They could be anything, amorphous black shapes now scattering across the sky, squeaking like metal on metal until they are so far away they make no sound at all. Iris takes a step back. The tree, she thinks, doesn't want her to come any closer. She closes her eyes and the wind turns colors in her mind— blue, purple, and finally black, and she can feel the tree's roots rushing beneath the ground under her feet, undulating darkly toward the house.

Suddenly she hears a clang, then a rattle, and opens her eyes to see a figure in shadow, scrabbling up over the chain link fence. She watches as the figure hops down and takes off running down the long dirt road, until whoever it is has vanished before her eyes, blended in with the night fog.

She wakes up on the floor, still wrapped like a mummy. The quilt is tight around her nose and mouth. Panicked, she fumbles for an opening in the covers and sucks in the cool night air, her body filmed over with sweat.

BRIGHT AND EARLY

It is now five in the morning on Friday, and Iris has climbed back into bed, but has not managed to get back to sleep. She lies still on her back to accommodate the crick in her neck, her knees still smarting from the fall. She swims her legs around in circles under the sheets, to loosen the blood, mentally infusing it with the power to quiet her whole self. But this is not sleep.

Outside, birds are beginning to chirp. She opens her eyes, blinks, and decides that this is as good a time as any to get up. She throws the covers off and heads for the shower, tripping over her shoes in the dark. By a quarter to six, she is dressed in a gray, knee-length skirt and a pale blue polyester blouse that looks almost like silk. She has tea and toast standing at the kitchen counter, watching the sky turn white outside the sliding glass door to her small balcony, which is bare save for some dry leaves and dirt, with a view overlooking the alley, where someone has spray painted "Lery— were's my money bitch" on the wall of the apartment building next door. Ready for the day a couple of hours too early, she leaves for work. She might as well. There is nowhere else she can think of to go.

Hers is not the only car on the road, but every few blocks or so she finds herself alone at an intersection, waiting on a red light at a corner that looks and feels abandoned, stores with metal enclosures locked, empty bus shelters. She turns off the radio, cutting off Rod Stewart on *I wish I'd never seen your face.*

Her eyes scan the desolate street and it feels like an aftermath to something she missed, as though everyone but she got the memo to evacuate, paper bags and soda cans like tumbleweeds skittering across the pavement. Then a car pulls up beside her and her white-knuckled giddiness wanes.

At the office, she gets the door unlocked, shuts off the burglar alarm, wanders from room to room flipping on all the fluorescent lights, turns on printers and copiers. The office fills with the sound of rebooting, mechanical buzzes and clicks. It is all but alive. Once the suite is aglow in that greenish wash that has come to look normal to her, it doesn't matter what time it is. Artificial light gives no clues. There is just one window to the outside that is visible from her desk, just before the hallway. The window sits fifteen feet off the ground, facing the street.

Iris hoists herself up on her desk between the phone and computer. This window has bothered her for some time, though she only noticed it a few months ago. Too high for anyone to look out of, she cannot imagine what it is for. And yet, it was planned, blueprinted and built this way, a non-window that she only assumes looks out on the street because there is nothing on the other side of the wall in which it sits. If she's figured right. It is not even seven, and her boss won't be in until at least nine. She wonders if there might be a custodian's closet somewhere in the building from which she might borrow a ladder. She could take full advantage of this time.

It occurs to her then, also, that she is definitely, unquestionably, the first person here. She is in a position to watch the door, see who shows up. She promises herself that she will pay attention today. Iris straightens her spine and rolls her shoulders forward and back. She stretches her arms upward, and at the moment she locks her fingers together over her head, a loud ringing shocks her onto her feet, and she thinks for one panicked second that she has caused it, nudged some invisible lever in the air. Her eyes dart around the room, looking for a source, until she realizes it is coming from outside the door. She inches toward the sound and listens as the ringing changes pattern after a minute, turning into a more insistent series of shrieks. Suddenly, the ringing stops and a distant, muffled male voice groans, "Fuuuuuuck…"

She opens the door a crack, and sees that there is no one in the hallway. Then she hears a radio switched on, barely audible news, traffic, weather, she can't tell— there are only bright voices talking fast, and her eyes settle on the closed door of suite 2B.

After a while, poised in the doorway like this, the voices on the radio lose the pattern of human speech. All she hears is a prolonged static hum, then she realizes the station has been changed, and what she hears is music, but it's so quiet, she can't detect a melody. She fixes her eyes on the wall and enters into a state of semi-consciousness, letting the eggshell color of the wall blend with the lavender carpet to form a gauzy absence of vision. She thinks she could stay like this, looking and not looking, hearing and not hearing, for ages.

So she is startled when the door opens, and the man from 2B emerges in T-shirt and sweatpants, his cheeks darkly bristled. What Iris sees is only a streak of him as he passes, his beige and black and whiteness bleeding through the haze of the hallway, but this is enough. He pauses for only a second in front of her door, though he doesn't turn to face her, and she pushes it swiftly shut. She stays where she is, her head against the door, and listens as he enters the restroom and shuts the door behind him.

Iris returns to her desk and switches her computer on. She imagines him then, in the bathroom, stripping naked and washing each individual body part in the shallow sink, drying himself with paper towels. Would he be able to wedge himself under the faucet to wash his back, his crotch? Does he drink water from the faucet too, or does he go without water, like a cactus, needing nothing? Her computer turns on with a languid ding and she has an impulse to get up and go back to his office while he is otherwise occupied, to steal something as evidence, or simply await his return. Then there is a knock at her door and she freezes, making no move to answer. She holds her breath, as though whoever has knocked might hear the difference.

"Hello?" comes her boss's voice, "are you in there? I forgot my key."

Iris exhales and jumps up to open the door for him. "It wasn't locked..." she starts as he steps through the doorway. He takes off his sunglasses and jacket and holds these to his chest.

"Why are you here so early?" she asks, flustered, as he passes her, heading down the hall.

"Why are you?" he says, before disappearing into his office.

Iris spends the rest of the morning with her ears perked up like a dog's, one focused inside, the other out. With her left ear, she listens for any movements in the hallway, but there is only the opening and closing of doors, and she can't tell if any of them have been opened or closed by the man from 2B. Her right ear is trained toward her boss's office, from which there has been no sound since he arrived. Her listening game collapses any time the phone rings. After transferring a call to her boss, she has to divide up her hearing all over again, which takes concentration. But nothing comes of it, and by lunchtime, she is ready to give up. She decides she will tackle the long-put-off file cabinet reorganization upon her return.

When she gets back, as she is tucking her leftover half-sandwich into the bottom drawer of her desk, she hears her boss's voice booming, loud enough that she can hear through his closed door, "Exactly! That's exactly what I said!"

Another voice responds then, but she can't make out the words, only the sound. She quickly approaches the office, trying to interpret the back and forth chattering, but thinks better of it. It wouldn't do to be caught holding a glass to the door.

She wants to stay and wait for the door to open, but she has to go to the bathroom. She hurries down the outside hall to the restroom and pees as fast as she can, washes her hands but doesn't bother drying them. She shakes them in the air as she hustles back to the office.

But her boss is standing in front of her desk when she returns.

"Hey, listen," he starts in immediately, "I need something from my car, but I can't leave just now. Will you get something for me?"

"What is it?"

"It's a box. It's rectangular. It's in the backseat."

"Uh, sure." And before she gets the words out, he's pressing a car key with its dangling remote into her palm.

He's too close to her all of a sudden, closer than she thinks they have ever been. She can see his pores, and the sparse blond chest hair peeking out the top of his striped dress shirt, and she takes a step back, avoiding his eyes, though she can't avoid his scent, a chaotic swirl of mint, soap, a steely cologne, something that would come in a silver bottle, and underneath it all, the unmistakable smell of sweat that is never really masked.

"Good good, thanks," he calls over his shoulder, and hustles back to his office.

In the parking lot, Iris's gaze falls on the white van a few spaces down from her boss's convertible. She glances around the lot before approaching it, but she finds that its windows are the tinted kind that block everything out. The windows must have been an add-on, because they don't match the beat-up exterior, they're so smooth and new-looking. She runs a finger along the dirty back door and chews on her bottom lip. *Windows used to be simpler*, she thinks. *Windows used to break.*

She sees that she has drawn a distinct line in the dirt, and without thinking, she picks it up again, running her finger all along the back, then slowly walking around to the side, dragging her finger just above the wheel wells, across the hood and back around, so a thin, shaky white line seems to divide the van into two horizontal pieces held together by a row of sharp teeth. She stands back and looks at it, surprised at her impulse, but it can't be undone now. She wipes her finger off on the inner hem of her skirt and backs away a few paces before retrieving the box from the convertible's open backseat, just sitting there, warm from the sun. She doesn't even need the key. The box is so light it could be empty, and she carries it under one arm back to the building.

Back in the office, she knocks on her boss's closed door. He doesn't answer.

She knocks again, and waits. When he doesn't answer the third knock, she opens the door to find nobody. He or they have slipped off somehow, in the two minutes she was outside. Was it longer than that? He must have gone the instant she disappeared down the stairs.

She feels momentarily compelled to open the box and empty its mystery contents onto the lavender carpet, but thinks better of it. Instead she sets it on his desk, with a brief note on top: *Here*, the keychain splayed out beside it.

The rest of the day passes slowly. There are no more phone calls. As the clock edges past three, she realizes just how long she has been here and feels like her mouth is drying out. She decides that if her boss comes back she will shoot him some kind of look. The office feels emptier than ever. Her knees bounce under the desk as she coils the phone cord around her index and middle fingers, uncoils it, coils it again. She listens in vain for the man next door, pictures him in homey scenarios: folding laundry, cooking dinner, falling asleep like a kitten, trying not to, his eyelids slipping, his head jerking up, resistant. It occurs to her that he could be asleep right now. She could open his door and find him curled up in the green chair, a line of drool glistening on his jaw. If she were to open the door.

She scoots her chair back against the wall, stands up, and

heads to the conference room. She pulls a fresh sheet of paper out of the fax machine and sits down at the big oak table, marker in hand.

Dear Neighbor, she begins.

Where are you, what do you, who, she writes quickly and instantly crosses it out.

I'm sorry, she begins, on a fresh sheet, but can't think of a way to finish the sentence, or why she has started it this way. *I'm sorry I'm sorry I* she writes before pushing it aside.

She lays out another, and stares at it for a long time. *What am I after*, she whispers out loud.

Dear you, she writes, slowly, deliberately, holding the paper tightly against the table.

What are you doing in there? All I want is to know.
—Next door

She folds the note into an envelope and writes *2B* on the back. She clutches the envelope in her hands until it is past five, then wonders if it's okay for her to go. There's been no sign of her boss, and his keys are still here. Finally, she decides that he must know what he's doing, and he can't expect her to do anything she wouldn't normally do. She turns everything off, all the lights, all electronics. She sets the alarm and locks up. In front of 2B, she gets down on her knees and slides the envelope underneath the door, listening to the paper as it crinkles against the soft, nubby carpet. She walks slowly toward the stairwell, still hoping that she will hear something, anything out of the ordinary, anything opening, closing, unlocking, beginning. She pauses at the top of the stairs before continuing down and out into the parking lot, where her boss's car still sits, a few spaces down from her own.

CONVENTION

Neil leans his chest against the hotel's front desk while the woman behind the counter fills a folder with pamphlets and maps and room service menus. He thinks of stopping her, of telling her he's only going to be here for twenty-four hours and is unlikely to stray beyond the convention halls and ballrooms on the lobby level— if he even makes it that far— but she's moving so quickly, her hands zipping and shuffling through the standard procedure that he can't bring himself to jump in. He see-saws back and forth on his heels, bouncing his chest lightly on the marble desk and back again, the height of it making him feel small, and a little ridiculous. The woman towers over him, brandishing her stapler, her keys on an elastic band around her wrist. He looks up at her like a bored child.

"Finch!" a voice calls out behind him, and a moment later, there's Mason slapping his back.

"Mason, how are you?"

"Good good, glad you decided to show this year."

"Yeah well, it's compulsory, isn't it?"

"Right, right."

The two look past each other, smiling their studied, mellow smiles, nodding at nothing, their tongues probing their back teeth.

"You check out the event schedule yet? I'm leading the 'Knowing the Consumer' talk this year. You should check it out— 4:30 in the main ballroom— there'll be hors d'oeuvres, shrimp I think, maybe some little sandwiches."

"Wouldn't miss it."

"Seriously though, it's something you should check out."

"Right," Neil says, still smiling, his eyes darting up to the woman behind the counter, still fussing papers about, "I will be there."

"Cool— hey and the mixer's at 8:30, in the lounge. You'll be there, right? They were asking about you last time. I told 'em you were sick." Mason laughs and Neil thinks he can see a cavity on one of his molars. He's reminded again, looking at Mason's weak chin and shaving nicks, though he's technically Neil's boss, that he's a few years younger. He tries to think of something jocular to say.

"Say, you think Beaudry'll be there?" Neil says, taking the folder and key card from the woman and picking up his bag, already edging his way to the elevators, though rooted enough, his toes just rising ever so slightly inside his shoes. "That guy owes me a drink."

"Ken Beaudry?" Mason squints back at Neil as he steps forward and hands the woman his credit card. "You didn't hear?"

"No, what?" He hears the elevator ding and has to mentally restrain himself from backing away and crossing the whole lobby to meet it before it's summoned away again.

"About the car accident?"

"No…"

"About three months ago? T-boned in a goddamn intersection. He walked away from it, but he refused to go to the hospital, said he was fine— dropped dead a few hours later. Internal bleeding." He annunciates *bleeding*, like it's a medical term Neil might not be familiar with.

Neil hears an elevator again, and he wonders how many there are, how fast they can move. He wonders what floor he's on, but doesn't want to open up his folder and look just now.

"Why… why didn't I know that?" he asks.

Mason shrugs, "I don't know. I thought everybody knew."

"Oh, I'm, uh… I'm really sorry to hear that."

"Terrible."

Mason gets his folder, and Neil hears the elevators dinging again, several at a time it sounds like now. It's like they never stop picking people up, dropping them off, up and down and up, plodding along.

"Well, I'll see you later, then?" Neil says, beginning his slow approach, though he still doesn't know just where he's going.

"Hold up, I'll come with you," Mason says, rolling his black suitcase behind him.

"Sure, great," Neil smiles.

Waiting for the elevator, they find that they're both on the fifteenth floor. They watch the numbers overhead as they light up one by one.

"Oh check it out— this is one of those hotels that has no thirteenth floor. I didn't know that was still a thing."

"This hotel was built in the fifties, if I remember correctly," Neil says. "It was a thing then."

"No shit?"

"This was where a lot of Motown artists always stayed when they passed through here— before it was bought out."

"Oh yeah? How do you know this stuff?"

Neil shrugs and gives Mason a weak half-smile, and keeps watching the numbers as they pass twelve and go straight to fourteen. When they land at fifteen, Neil makes sure to get out first, mildly annoyed as Mason keeps walking right alongside him.

"It's gonna be a good time, man," Mason says, stopping at his door, "but don't get too wasted tonight— 'The Tao of the Sale' is at 8:00 a.m. Hey, see you down there."

Neil nods back to him and laughs, though nothing's funny. It just comes out, some kind of hiccup of good cheer. He continues on to his own room, feeling suddenly odd about being so high up. The windows he can see at the far end of the hall don't look out at anything. It's just grayish white sky. The hallway is so wide, and he drags his feet a little against the brown and darker brown checked carpet, spotting stains as he goes. He imagines for an instant that the whole hotel is empty, that it's just him rattling through the arid halls.

When he gets to his own room, he throws his things on the floor and sits on the tightly made hotel bed, across from an abstract portrait of a violin, its pieces broken apart in right angles, but hovering over a hazy ochre backdrop. He wonders how much something like that costs. Did it come from some big box store, from a bin next to the picture frames, or is there an artist somewhere who's cornered the dull hotel art market? He gets up and examines the painting for a signature, but finds none.

Over the bed is another one, a portrait of some fishing village done in the Impressionist style, little blotchy fishermen by a big blotchy sea, surrounded by smudgy little huts, the whole tableau bathed in the persistent sunlight creeping in through the Venetian blinds. He notices it isn't centered, and lifts up an edge with his index finger, finding a jagged circle of chipped paint on the wall behind it.

He's hit with a wave of fatigue, and lies down on the bed. He grabs the end of the bedspread and drapes it over himself, rolling up like a caterpillar. In the darkness, he breathes in its smell. He saw an exposé on TV late one night, where they passed blacklights over the bedding at several top hotel chains, revealing every variety of bodily fluid in harsh neon splatters. They found dust mites in the pillowcases, bed bugs teeming under the mattresses. The host wore rubber gloves.

He sits up quickly and checks his watch, then pulls the event schedule out of his folder. He has fifteen minutes before the "Sales Strategy Symposium." He'll be expected to talk at this one, so he needs time to get into the right mode. He goes over to the mirror above the dresser and looks at himself. He smiles, then tones it down to a half-smile.

"Hi," he mouths. "Good, good," "Good to see you," "Is that right?"

He raises his eyebrows and tilts his head. "Huh," he mouths, "that's something." "Me?" "Oh, good, good."

He clears his throat then and leans back a little, folding his arms. Out loud, he says, "Well I've always believed that the key to success is to sell the buyer's ideas back to him."

He shifts his stance. "That's very true," he says to the mirror, "but how do we sustain the buyer's enthusiasm once we've built it to the desired level?"

He closes his eyes and rolls his neck back and forth. He looks back to his reflection. He stands up straight, puffing out his chest a little, then smiles again, mentally complimenting himself on the whiteness of his teeth. He locks his focus onto the reflection of his pupils with some vague idea of fishing himself out. When his own gaze starts to feel too hard, he closes his eyes and visualizes his body filling up with bubbles, light as air. With each breath, he visualizes the bubbles rising up toward the top of his head. He smoothes his hair, pops a breath mint, and makes for the door.

Neil has stayed in hundreds of hotels, and the bedding always feels fresh and blank, and smells like the package it came in. There's not a thing wrong with it. Why, he wonders, is everyone always on the lookout for something to be wrong?

Sunday

Summer has barely begun, and already, the air is growing thick. Iris lies by the rooftop pool of Mallory's apartment complex. This is a ritual they have carried over from their college days, only nobody had a pool then, so they would sneak into hotels posing as guests. But there was no sneaking or posing necessary. No one ever questioned them. No one ever said a word, and why should they— to a couple of girls at the pool? Now they lie on their backs, virtually synchronized in their cigarette drags and iced coffee sips. Up here, the sun feels closer, the air more molten. They are the only ones here, ten stories above the afternoon bustle.

"Oh hey," Mallory says, "did you ever go out with that guy? The one from my party?" She sits up and twists her wet hair into an intricate knot, then lets it fall forward over one shoulder.

"Who?" Iris asks, half listening. Her eyes are closed, and she concentrates on the orange wash behind her eyelids.

"You know…" Mallory says, easing back down into her chair.

"Oh. Yeah."

"You sound enthusiastic. What was the matter with him? Didn't like the sound of his footsteps? Thought his teeth were too straight?" Mallory cackles and takes a drag.

"I don't know. I got sort of drunk and I don't remember what I said to him. I think I might have been a little mean."

"He said you were 'cryptic'."

"So you already knew. You weren't even asking a question." Iris opens her eyes and squints into the light.

"Sorry, I just thought that was a funny thing for him to say. Did you like him at all?"

Iris shrugs and tosses her cigarette butt into her emptied cup, the ice hushing its spark. "I don't remember."

Mallory laughs. "That's what I'm gonna start doing," she says. "Any time someone asks me a question. Feign amnesia to shut people up." She smiles and slips down further into the chair.

"I'm not feigning," Iris laughs, "I couldn't name one thing we talked about."

Mallory sighs and rolls over onto her side, facing away from Iris. "That's some talent," she yawns. "You must work at it." A minute later, she begins to snore softly, a low whispered growl.

Iris closes her eyes and flirts with the idea of sleep, the sun pushing its way under her skin and massaging her bones. Her every joint bursts with dozy warmth. She feels the sun's rays as one solid mass that pushes her untanned flesh further into the deck chair, causing her body to sink and spread, liquid contained only by a black bikini. She takes off her sunglasses and gets up out of the chair, and the sun turns its attention elsewhere.

She steps into the pool, heated so there is hardly any difference between air and water. It is just a change in texture, a hazy barrier between dry and slick. When she is all the way in, she drifts toward the center where the water is deepest, and leans her head back, letting her legs float to the surface. Then she turns over and pushes her way down to the bottom. She stays down there, stroking her fingers against the soft concrete, bobbing up an inch, then pushing down again. She listens to the underwater echo of nothing— nothing out nothing in. When she can't hold her breath any longer, she floats up and emerges with a subdued splash. She pushes her hair back, and watches as an elderly woman enters the pool area with two small boys trailing behind her. They are engaged in water gunplay, babbling threats in their tiny animal voices. The woman, in a floral, skirted swimsuit, spreads a towel out on one of the deck chairs and lies down, placing a giant straw hat over her face. Iris wonders then if the boys are with her at all, as they drop their weapons and hop into the shallow end. She climbs out the other side and drips her way over to the edge of the roof. She leans against the concrete enclosure and wrings her hair out over the edge, hoping to see the water hit the sidewalk, but it gets lost somewhere along the way, caught in the air. She parts her lips slightly and takes a deep breath, but she doesn't feel like she's taken anything in.

Just then, she hears a yelp, and turns to see Mallory sitting up in her chair. She goes over and finds her frantically picking up her purse, flip flops, cup, keys, as though looking for something underneath them.

"Fuck," Mallory says. "How long was I asleep? What time is it?"

Across the pool, one of the boys lets out a scream that collapses into a hysterical laugh.

"I don't know," Iris says, "let's go now."

Space

Iris's alarm goes off at a quarter to six. She tries to shower quickly, but her daydreams are persistent. She is on a Ferris wheel overlooking the Grand Canyon when suddenly the wheel comes off its hinges and hurdles forward into the dusty maw. Everyone is screaming, their hands gripping the sides of their candy-colored compartments. But the screaming stops as, one by one, they all notice that they have been hovering over the canyon for some time, the air acting as a cushion on which the Ferris wheel rests. She comes to with shampoo dripping down her face. She leans her head back into the spray to rinse it all out, lets the water run down over her skin before shutting it off and spitting into the drain. She dresses simply, in a black cotton sleeveless dress, and is in the car at six-thirty, leaving the windows open to air dry her hair.

Once at the office, she starts up the day's machinery, pressing buttons with a decisive index finger, one by one.

She waits. She listens to voicemail and writes down her boss's one message, which she then leaves on top of a pile of unopened mail on his desk: *Mr. Farquar(sp?) called. He needs you to call him back ASAP because he is "at the end of his rope." No number.*

Then she hears what she has been waiting for, the angry mechanical bleat of the alarm followed by the smack and the mumbled profanities, then the crackle of voices on the radio. She moves toward the door and presses her ear against it, creating a seal, a small private space between her head and the building. She imagines him shuffling about in a bathrobe, scratching his unshaven face and kicking things that get in his way. Or he could still be in bed. Or doing any other thing one might imagine. She shouldn't get ahead of herself. But in her head, in that sealed space between her ear and the door, she can feel his awakening as a cloud that fills his room, and sends cold vibrations through the doors and around her body, circling.

She stands like this, waiting, but nothing follows. She never hears the door open, or anything else. She wonders if he even got the note. If she even really left it. Maybe she could still take it back. Finally, she sits down at her desk and turns on her computer. There won't be anything today. She tells herself this. When the doorknob turns, though she is doing nothing wrong, she snaps to attention, puts on a serious look, and squints at her computer screen.

"Good morning," she offers, looking up as her boss enters the room.

"If you can call it that," he mutters, rapping her desk with his knuckles as he passes.

Box

Several days later, Iris arrives at the office to find a box on her desk. She sees it as soon as she turns on the lights, and stares at it while she de-activates the alarm system. She drops her purse beside her desk and looks at it from the side. It is about the size of a brick, and has been taped so thoroughly, so determinedly that it shines like liquid. She is almost afraid to touch it. She keeps her eyes locked on it as she turns on her computer and checks voicemail, as though she thinks it will vanish if she looks away.

When she can't stall any longer, she picks it up. It is light as a piece of paper. With a letter opener, she stabs a thin line around the edges, and lifts off the top of the box like a lid. Inside, there is a white paper napkin folded in half. She opens it, and inside are written the words, *I am very busy. Don't ask. Ask me later. I'm not here.*

Nameless

Iris learned what death was when she was six years old. She had been sitting at the kitchen table, eating cereal on a Saturday morning, her bare feet resting on Sebastian. She laid her feet on the coarse hair of his back, and he kept her from dangling. Her cereal had gone soggy— she couldn't eat it fast enough. She was watching the shredded wheat change properties while her mother stood at the counter, scraping oatmeal from the sides of the pot into a white bowl.

On the radio, they were talking about a famous singer whose death from an undiagnosed heart defect had just been announced. He had been found slumped over his kitchen table by the housekeeper. The host was taking calls from people who said they had always felt a connection with him, and people who, embarrassed, admitted he was their first crush. One woman, who readily admitted she was old enough to have been his mother, broke down on the air.

She gasped and heaved for ten seconds straight, the host intermittently whispering, "It's okay… it's okay…"

When she finally regained composure, she apologized.

"Oh god, I don't know why I'm reacting so strongly to this. I feel like an idiot. I don't even know why I called you."

"You're not an idiot," the host said. "It's a sad day. For all of us, and especially for those of us who loved his songs so much.

We'll be back after these words. You're listening to KSTR, the star of the airwaves."

Iris was confused. She stared into the mush in her cereal bowl and listened as the somber mood of the broadcast was overturned by a bright jingle for a carpet cleaning company. She was jarred by the sound of the twinkling piano and the chorus of voices, singing a phone number, all in unison. Suddenly, she felt like gagging, as though hair were growing on the inside of her throat.

She looked to her mother to see if she too had noticed the change, or if it was only her, but her mother never looked away from the window. Iris poked her head under the table to let Sebastian know she was leaving the table. She made eye contact with him and swiveled around in her chair, lightly dropping her feet on the linoleum. He got up and followed her down the hall to her bedroom.

She was sitting on the floor of her room, adjusting the Velcro flaps of her tennis shoes, attempting to reach the perfect level of tightness. Each time she affixed them, she stopped, concentrated on the space or lack thereof inside her shoes, then tried again. Sebastian sat in the center of the doorway. Then Neil called from the front door, "Hey dingleberry— we're going to the lagoon without you if you don't hurry up!"

Iris jumped up, ran down the hall to him, waving goodbye as she passed the kitchen, though her mother wasn't there to receive it, having already disappeared into some other corner of the house.

The lagoon was a mile away. Iris, her brother, and their father walked in a line, three abreast along the gravel road, Sebastian trotting ahead, alongside little houses just like theirs, great yards, trees, and pastures hidden behind. Iris looked at each house, hoping to see glimpses of the neighbors through their windows. They had only moved there several weeks earlier, at the start of the summer, and Iris still didn't have a handle on who lived where. She had noticed people from afar, but hadn't spoken to any of them. It was such a small town, she thought she ought to have it memorized by now, but it was a hard thing to do, alone in her mind. Her favorite thing about this place was the horses that had come with the house. She could talk to them for hours, leaning her cheek against the fence between the backyard and corral. After so many afternoons spent baking in the sun like that, their previous residence had all but completely slipped from her memory.

She turned her gaze forward again. Their shadows were tall and limber, like licorice whips. She imagined that the four of them were cowboys on some kind of mission. It was so quiet out, and the sun was so bright that Iris had to look at the ground, holding her father's giant hand and listening to the gravel crunching under their feet.

When they reached the path that circled the lagoon, Neil ran ahead, following Sebastian into the high cattails by the edge of the murky green water. Ducks congregated nearby. Iris continued holding onto her father's hand, wind now blowing her ponytail into her face.

After a long moment in which she tried to think of the best way to ask the question that had been brewing all morning in the bottom layer of her mind, she blurted out, "He's dead."

"What?" her father said, squinting down at her.

She shook her head and continued.

"The singer. On the radio... they said he's dead. Is he?"

"That's right," he said, squeezing her hand a little tighter.

They continued walking down the path, watching as Neil grabbed a fistful of cattails and crushed them in his grip. He threw the dust in the air and Sebastian leapt after it, catching bits on his face and on the tip of his big lolling tongue, while Neil snapped off another one, laughing.

"But, what happens now?" she continued, looking up at her

father's rough jawline, and the pallor of his throat, a dark red razor nick just above his Adam's apple, "You know, until…"

"Hmm? What was that?"

"What happens?"

"Well," he started, "his family is very sad right now. He was too young. But…" he stopped walking now and looked down into her face. "It's not something you have to worry about, okay?"

"No," she sighed, exasperated, "I mean what happens until he comes back."

"What?"

"How long is he dead for? Where does he go?"

"Iris," he said, crouching down in front of her, holding her small, seemingly boneless arm in his hand. Her father's eyes searched her face, and she felt exposed, opened against her will. She wanted to hide whatever he was looking for, to bury it within the maze of her guts and nerves. She turned her head toward the ground, a line of ants wending their way out of the patchy grass to her right and onto the dirt path. It struck her then that the ants knew exactly where they were going and what they were doing, always.

"Hey," he said, gently pulling her face back toward him, "we never… your mom never told you?" He looked worried, his eyes racing across her face.

Iris ran her shoe back and forth in the dirt.

"Honey, people don't come back after they die."

"They do…" she murmured.

"No… who told you that?"

"I know they don't always, but sometimes they… don't they?" she tried, backtracking. She wished she had never said anything. She couldn't remember what she'd expected him to say.

"Oh, honey," he sighed, and the pity in his eyes— she recognized it.

Another gust of wind blew dust into their faces. Her father let go of her arm and coughed, and Iris started running.

The sleepy willow trees, the white sun, the thick cattails and green water— they were all just streaks of color against her low sky. She was running so fast her senses couldn't keep up. Her whole body was knotted up in her pulsing lungs. When she couldn't run any further, she slumped down into a patch of grass. She rolled over onto her back and closed her eyes, imagining she was underneath it. She breathed heavily, trying to feel what it would be like to be dead. But she couldn't feel it. Even with her eyes closed, there were so many things happening. There was warmth, there was the scratching of the dry grass on her arms and the backs of her calves. There was the sound of the wind. There were her own sounds, too— her breath, the sound of her hands clutching at the grass, and always, always some song singing itself in her head— silently humming in spite of her efforts to be still.

She opened her eyes when she felt Sebastian's tongue on her cheek. Her father and Neil were on their knees on either side of her. Sebastian had been swimming in the lagoon. He dripped the slimy water down her neck as he buried his face behind her ear, like he was going to gobble her whole. She wanted to stay right there for as long as she could, as long as they would let her. She would will time to stop for her. All those dead people, she decided, they just didn't want it enough.

As her father carried her away, she buried her face into his shoulder and made a promise to herself, to want the world with all her heart. She looked back and saw Neil lagging behind, soberly watching his own shadow extending out across the dirt road, while Sebastian ran up in front of them, leading them all back home.

Sometimes, Iris will forget all about that day for years at a time. When it comes back to her, like heat in her veins, she does not know what to call it. She is mute with desire, and dread.

HERE AND NOT HERE

I'm very busy. Don't ask. Ask me later. I'm not here.

She runs her fingers over the words, then folds up the napkin and tucks it into a zippered pocket of her purse. She crushes the box and stuffs it into the wastebasket, quickly, instinctively, as though destroying evidence.

Still operating on instinct, her motions swift and mechanical, she pulls a blank sheet of paper out of her desk drawer, uncaps her marker and writes, *But you are here. I see you. And it's later already.*

She folds the note into thirds and steps out of the office, but facing 2B, she stops. She wants him to find it, but not to see it coming. She imagines him on the other side of the door, watching as the note slides across the carpet. She imagines him picking it up and dropping it into the trash, unread. She imagines him never even looking down.

She turns and rushes down the stairs, pushes the door open and strides across the parking lot to where the white van sits, the remnants of her fingered outline still lightly etched in the dirt. Standing in the weedy grass behind the curb, facing the van head on, she sees now how hulking it is, how mammoth and forbidding. She lifts one knee up onto the van, then the other, so she is facing the windshield, her palms pressed against the hood, still cold from the long night. She unfolds the note and crawls up closer, pressing it to the glass so it faces the driver's seat. She fastens it with the windshield wiper, which leaves a gray line down the meat of her hand.

She stays there a moment, on all fours, facing the darkened windshield, the inside blocked off from the outside gaze. *He could be in there*, she thinks. *He could be looking right at me, and I wouldn't know the difference.*

"Hello," she mouths, looking straight ahead into the opaque window, before hopping down and jogging back to the building. She stops at the door to brush off her dirtied knees and shins.

Corporate Talking

Days go by. Her boss is gone again; she doesn't know when he'll be back. She asks him once, when he calls with instructions to re-type and mail an email he has sent her.

"Do you know what day you'll be back? By the end of this week, you think?"

"Hard to say, hard to say," he says, trailing off, "it's just hard to say at this point…"

This is enough to tell her that— for the time being, she doesn't have to worry about being caught as she continues to come in early, and to stare out into the hallway, waiting. Sometimes she waits a long time and the man never comes out. She knows he got the note she left on his van— because it's gone. Unless the wind carried it off. Unless someone else took it. He must come out sometimes— she's noticed the van's shifting position in the parking lot. Someone is moving. She wonders if he is well stocked on supplies, if the room is some kind of above-ground bomb shelter. Maybe he is an agoraphobic. It eventually occurs to her that she might hear more if she stations herself at the wall shared by the two offices, behind a sloping, lopsided desk in the storage room. With its musty darkness, and its piles of broken appliances and clutter, it looks as though the bomb has already hit. Iris flicks on the light and squeezes in between an ancient Xerox machine and a dented file cabinet to get to the wall.

She doesn't know how he got into her office to leave her the note, but despite his stillness, she has come to believe that he is capable of anything. The least he can do now is to make some noise— a snore, a sigh— anything to feed her wonder.

On the days he complies, with the scoot of a chair, a hearty yawn, or a coughing fit, she feels his presence on the other side all day long. Even the sleepy sound of his classical radio is enough. She is typing and she imagines he is combing his hair. She is filing, and he is making a sandwich. While she is standing in front of the fax machine, watching it crank out a sheet of paper in fits and starts, he is doing tai chi, arms outstretched, left foot pointed, toes first, toward the closed window, breathing in the same recycled air. If it weren't for the wall, they would inhabit the same space, entirely. She wonders if he knows this.

On the days she hears nothing, she imagines that he has packed up and disappeared. She checks every morning to make sure the white van is still in the parking lot, but it could be a different white van, there are other white vans— she never did take note of the license plate number. Or maybe he is still asleep, she tells herself, maybe he is asleep and dreaming of air, his body slumped over in the green chair or conked out on the floor, his consciousness floating just outside, between the thin, viscous clouds.

It's not enough.

On a Friday morning at eight o'clock, Iris decides to knock on his door. She convinces herself to do it by imagining the worst that could happen. The worst that could happen is that he won't answer, she decides, and she already knows what that's like. She does not think about the best thing that could happen. She doesn't get that far.

So she steps out into the hallway, taking care not to lock her own door behind her as she does not bring her keys. She reaches out her hand and knocks one time, pauses, then three quick knocks, like a stuttered exclamation point. And then she waits.

She counts thirty seconds and knocks again. She hears a

thump and what sounds like a rustling of fabric. He is in there, somebody is. Or he has escaped out the window, letting the drapes fly in the breeze, knocking blunt objects off of tables. But still no answer.

"Hello?" she finally says. The rustling stops.

"Hello?" she repeats, having again arrived at thirty-Mississippi in her head.

When he fails, still, to respond, she talks to the door.

"Was the note I got— the one in the box— was it you?" She thinks then that she should have brought it as some kind of visual aid, but it is at home, on top of her dresser. She could slide it under the door to jog his memory, but then she might not get it back.

"Hello," she tries again, more quietly this time, "I answered it. Did you see that I wrote back?"

She knocks again, just two quick taps, and before she has even retracted her fist, the door opens a crack. The man brings his face forward into the opening and looks at Iris. His eyes are half closed, with puffy bags underneath. She takes a step back.

"Hmm?" he whimpers. She understands now that she has woken him and she can't remember, suddenly, what was so urgent, what she expects him to do or say.

"Um..." she starts, "I was just asking if... I just wanted to... to introduce myself." She reaches out a limp hand, and they both look down at it wavering slightly in the dim light of the hallway.

He pauses before opening the door a little wider, his posture protective. His feet are bare, and he is wrapped in a white quilt, thick black hair exposed on his shins.

"Pleased to meet you," he says, his hands clasped inside the quilt so he is cocooned.

Iris drops her hand down to her side.

"So..." she says.

"What?"

"So... I asked you something, and I was just curious, I guess."

"I'm sorry— I don't follow," he says, his eyes darting between her face and the hallway behind her.

"I asked, and then you said don't ask."

"I don't know what you mean," he says.

"And then I said— it was you, wasn't it? Isn't that your van outside?"

"Uh…"

"I'm sorry, I should just go," Iris stammers. "I don't know what I'm asking you for. Forget I said anything, just forget…" she trails off, watches the man's face as he sucks in his cheeks and looks up at the stucco ceiling. She takes a moment to look past him and into the room. There are boxes overflowing with papers, furniture half assembled, metal scraps laid out on a tarp. He *is* busy, she thinks. There is a new addition, too, a Murphy bed, its thin white sheets softly rumpled, like little milky waves she can imagine sinking into, sinking until she disappears. Flip a switch and into the wall she would go.

"No, I'm sorry," he says, and she re-focuses on his face, his cloudy eyes and greasy hair. "Sorry I couldn't be of any help."

He begins to shut the door then, but stops. He reaches a hand out and touches Iris's arm, startling her. His hand is warm, his long knobby fingers light against her bare skin.

"Please don't mention this to anyone. Not for now, all right?"

He pulls his hand away and Iris folds her arms.

"Mention what?"

He smiles and nods slowly, then shuts the door, and she hears the click of a lock turning.

She stands paralyzed for a long moment before slipping down the hall to the ladies' room. She places her hands on either side of the white porcelain sink. The greenish overhead light makes her hands appear old, veiny, and dry. Or maybe it is the softer light in other rooms that makes them appear young and soft. She runs her left hand over the back of her right and it feels neither rough nor soft. It is too familiar. It is just her skin.

She looks into her reflection. The circles under her eyes are dark, maybe even darker than usual. She looks into her own eyes and tries to determine her expression. What is her face saying? Like her skin, it is too familiar for her to know, for her to even see it.

She thinks about the original note. *I am very busy. Don't ask. Ask me later. I'm not here.* If not him, then who? Is he lying, or is there something that escapes her? Is there any reason, she wonders, for her to think anything she thinks? What makes her decide anything? What is it that she thinks she knows? She washes her hands in cold water, running them around and around and around each other in pink liquid soap, and when she rinses them, she turns the faucet to warm. She holds her hands there until she stops feeling the water, and dries them under the air dryer. She watches the water droplets scatter across the backs of her hands.

When she returns from the bathroom, the door is open, and her boss is standing in the doorway, briefcase in hand.

"I just walked in and there was nobody here. The door was unlocked. I just walked in. That doesn't seem right to me, does it seem right to you?" he says.

"I'm sorry," she starts, "I just stepped out for a second."

"What time is it? When did you get here anyway?" She notices then that he is blocking her way in.

"I just… I woke up early. I thought I'd come in and just, get a head start…"

"Oh," he says. "Huh." He squints at her. Then he turns and enters the office. She follows.

"Listen, I have some things I need you to do for me," he calls over his shoulder. "I've got a big, big, big meeting in the conference room in one hour. I need bottled water, pens, coffee, the works."

He stops at his office door and turns back to her. "Hold on. Hold on a sec." He steps inside and closes the door behind him.

She stands there for a minute, poised and ready, before finally giving up and returning to her desk.

Iris begins a data entry project left over from the day before. Transferring numbers from one spreadsheet to another, she falls into a rhythm. Twos and eights and fives lose meaning, becoming shapes, configurations of curves and lines. She holds a pen between her teeth as she moves her mouse back and forth across the mouse pad. The taste of plastic in her mouth helps her focus.

Then her computer makes a twinkling sound. Mail. She sits up straight. She opens her email box and a new message from her boss sits in bold at the top of the list. She glances back in the direction of his office and clicks it open:

Please don't come in before 9:00am. And please don't stay after 5:00pm. There is a way things are supposed to look. Surprises aren't good. This is corporate talking. This isn't me talking.

As she finishes reading, a new message twinkles from the computer's small speakers. Again, from the boss, no subject:

This is what I need from you:

One dozen black ballpoint pens. Black or blue. Make it blue. If they don't come in denominations of a dozen, get ten or twenty.

One dozen bottles of water. Same as above re: denominations.

One dozen cups of black coffee. Separate cups— not those big jug things— this isn't a cafeteria. This may require several trips.

One dozen everything bagels. If they don't have everything get onion.

As she reads this, her boss approaches her desk. She looks up and he hands her a credit card.

"You'd better go now," he says. "I have to prepare my presentation."

Iris grabs her purse and her boss opens the door for her. In the doorway, he stops her, touching her elbow.

"Receipts for everything, okay?"

Just then, the door to 2B opens up and the man steps out, dressed now, uniform-like in a white dress shirt and black pants. His eyes dart back and forth between Iris and her boss and he glides quickly past them, head down. Iris watches her boss's eyes follow the man to the stairs, then snap back to her.

"Okay— be quick," he says, then steps back into the office and shuts the door.

Iris hurries down the stairs and out the door just in time to see the white van pull out and turn right out of the driveway. She imagines that if she hurried, she could catch up to him, but she stops herself. Her life turning into a James Bond film just doesn't seem like a plausible scenario. As Iris starts her car, she feels a headache coming on. She massages the space between her eyebrows, roughly, as though burrowing through the skin and into the pain's center, and heads for the drugstore.

At the store, she picks up a case of water, a box of pens. It occurs to her that they probably already have pens in the supply closet, but she didn't get a chance to look. In line at the checkout, Iris wonders just who her boss is meeting with. It's been some time since the conference room has gotten any use. In the past, this was routine. The conference room had gravitas. It was to be tiptoed past once she had set up, and the meeting was in full swing. Her boss would wait in his office until everyone had arrived, Iris seating them and offering beverages. When people started to get impatient, Iris was instructed to knock twice, softly, as a signal that he should make his entrance. There was fun in it, she has to admit, like playing a part. Then the door would close, and what went on inside— it wasn't her job to know. But how long has it been? She can't remember the last time she felt truly useful. As the cashier rings up her purchases, Iris begins to get excited. She never knew who he was meeting with, so what does it matter now?

Iris then drives to the café, loads her trunk with cardboard trays of coffee, tops securely fastened, a white box full of bagels. She drives so slowly back to the office that people honk and yell at her from their car windows, but she doesn't care. She is intent on not jostling anything. She eases into her parking spot so smoothly, she is liquid, the car is liquid, she is right on top of everything.

She starts by carrying one tray of coffee up to the office, balancing it carefully as she contends with the door. She approaches the conference room to begin setting up and finds a slip of paper on the round oak table:

Meeting moved off-site— last minute— talk next week— mea culpa.

Iris sets the tray down and sits. She pops the top off one of the coffees and drinks. She still has the credit card, she thinks. She could buy a ticket somewhere, to another state, another country. She could buy a boat, wherever one buys boats. She could just grab things and start buying them, how much for the streetlight, for the fire hydrant? She wonders if she could drink all of this coffee herself before it gets cold. She decides to try. She sits at the conference room table, drinking coffee until her blood is replaced by a continuous electric current, with no mass or volume at all.

Power Line

At the end of the day, Iris locks up the empty office. She leaves the coffee cups and bagels she nibbled for lunch on the conference room table. No one will see the mess. She'll be the one to clean it up anyway. As she goes from room to room, turning things off, she notices things are a little... dingier than she thinks they used to be. There are smudges on doorknobs, a thin layer of dust on the carpet, and the wastebaskets haven't been emptied recently. She remembers, just the other day, having lowered her foot into the trash, stamping it down to make room for more. *When does the custodian come*, she wonders. She can't remember when she last saw him in the early evening, with his cart lined with spray bottles in holsters. She wonders, too, what would happen if he didn't come anymore. How long would it take for filth to accumulate, and what if she started cleaning the place every day instead of answering the phone? Would her boss notice if she became the housekeeper instead of the receptionist? Would she, if it happened very gradually? She descends the darkened staircase and is out the door.

In the parking lot, she notes that the van is still gone, or gone again, and an instant later, she notices something on her windshield in the distance. She quickens her pace to the car and plucks a piece of thin brown paper out from under her windshield wiper. She opens her door and turns on the overhead light to read the penciled message:

It is later, and I'm not here. But you are.

She shoves the note into her glove compartment and looks around. She is alone. She starts the car and pulls out of the lot, confounded.

At red lights, she pulls the note out and re-reads it. She tries to remember if the handwriting matches the original note. Again, she asks herself, *what am I after?* She can't with any certainty say what she could possibly want. She shoves the note away again, covering it up with a pile of CDs, and when she parks the car at home, she leaves it there.

She enters her apartment, mail in hand. She sifts through it and pulls out a power bill. The rest she drops in the kitchen trash. Her hunger is urgent, her whole body knotted, steeped in acid. She opens the cabinet over the sink and scans its contents: spaghetti, canned tuna, minestrone, Ziploc bags, and light bulbs. She settles on the soup and heats it in a small saucepan. While the minestrone swirls over the heat of the blue flame, Iris turns on the oldies station. They're playing that song, *they're coming to take me away ha ha they're coming to take me away*, whatever it's called, whoever it's by. She hates gag songs, finds them disingenuous and unfunny, but she leaves it, expecting something better to follow. As she watches the soup begin to bubble, "Get Off My Cloud" comes on. Iris pours the soup into a white ceramic bowl. She turns off the burner, then turns it on and off again, checking, before crushing several saltine crackers into the bowl. She turns the radio up as she carries her soup out to the balcony, leaving the sliding door open. Some graffiti has been added to the opposite wall. Now, beneath the "Lery— were's my money bitch" is some kind of signature, a star with an anarchy symbol jammed clumsily into its center.

She is impatient, and begins eating while the soup is still nearly scalding, but it is not so bad. She knows there is pleasure in the burnt tongue feeling she will have for the rest of the night. The numbness will make her feel invincible, capable of swallowing swords. She eats looking out at her street. In front of her, fifty feet away at her fourth floor level, a pair of electric blue sneakers hangs from the power line. She thinks they are a new addition, but can't say for sure. She wonders how they got up so high. How many tries did it take, and where was she for the trying? Who spent a night hurling shoes up into the sky, hoping to catch something, settling, finally, for the power line?

"Get Off My Cloud" fades out and into "Open My Eyes" by The Nazz, and she thinks of what she might throw and where it might land.

When she gets to sleep, well after midnight, she sleeps deeply and long. Her dreams are not stories, but images one after another: droplets of condensation swelling on a glass of lemonade. Windmills clustered together on a yellow hill, spinning faster and faster, endlessly. A dry leaf on the sidewalk. A child's thumb crushing it, grinding back and forth. A line of ants snaking across the bottom of an empty motel swimming pool. A rusted-out car in the middle of the desert. The sun, a runny yolk in the sky, dripping onto red dirt, little by little until there is nothing left of it, the sky extinguished as the last drop hits.

Birthday

Iris wakes up panting. She gets a handle on it, breathing slowly and deliberately, any vague memory of her dreams escaping little by little with each passing moment. It is Saturday, and she guesses by the depth of sunlight oozing through her window that the day has unfolded itself already without her. She sits up and looks at the clock on her bedside table. It is just after one o'clock. She is groggy, hung over from too much sleep. She drops her feet heavily onto the floor and blinks, letting her eyes adjust to the waking world.

The phone rings and Iris squints around the room. She walks out into the hallway, following the sound, and finds the phone on its charger on the kitchen wall.

"Hello?"

"Happy Birthday, sweetheart. You sound groggy. Were you napping?"

"Oh, Mom, hi. No, I was awake."

Her mother's voice is low and soft. It makes no exclamations. Iris is disoriented, realizing all at once that it is in fact her birthday, and that it has been a while, two months at least, since she has spoken to either of her parents.

"Any special plans?"

"Oh, I hadn't really thought about it. I don't really know."

She hears the faint sounds of barking on the other end.

"Marvin," her mother whispers, "Marvin, honestly."

"How is Marvin?"

Marvin is the dog that came after Sebastian, an identical German shepherd. Though she knows he is a different dog, Iris, on the few occasions that she has seen Marvin, pretends that he is the same, imagining a long-shared history. She figures that it makes no difference to him what relationship she privately imposes.

"Cranky as ever. I thought we had gotten through the puppy stage, but he is still quite a little brat. That's right, Marvin," she murmurs away from the receiver, "I called you a brat."

Iris smiles.

"So, you're twenty-five now," her mother says suddenly. "That's the age I was when I married your father. I don't mean that to pressure you— it's just an observation. Actually, it seems an appallingly young age to me now. Just in general."

"I don't feel any pressure."

"Good. I don't want you to feel any pressure to do anything, ever."

"I don't."

"That's good."

The two stand on opposite ends of the phone line, several hundred miles between them, each standing in the same pose, bent sideways, right elbow resting on kitchen counter, left hand holding receiver.

"Your father says happy birthday. He mouthed it to me. He just stepped out— taking some stuff to the Goodwill."

"Oh. Tell him thank you."

"I will." Her mother pauses. Iris pauses with her.

"How's the new place?"

"Oh well—" her mother sighs, "I'll tell you what... it's just too big for the two of us. It's just too much."

"Really? Isn't it like, an apartment? Two bedrooms, you said, right?"

"I don't know... it's just not... well there's still so much *space* to think about. I never know where to go, where to find anything. But don't worry about it— I promise we'll tell you when we move again." She laughs a quick, throaty laugh.

"Oh…" Iris says, remembering the move before this one, when they failed to share their new address with her until they'd been there a month and a half, after the Father's Day card she'd sent to their old address came back marked return to sender.

"Are you well?" Her mother says abruptly, "would you tell me if you weren't?"

"Sure, yeah."

"Okay. Well. I don't want to keep you any longer. Have a wonderful day, sweetheart."

"Thank you."

They hang up without goodbyes.

Iris sets the phone down and considers her kitchen counter. It is the same pattern linoleum as the floor, as though the contractor finished the floor of pale yellow squares, shrugged, and kept going. She scratches at a dark spot on the tile, a stain of indeterminate origin, but it is ingrained.

She thinks back over the past week, tries to remember writing down any dates or glancing at any calendars. The approaching date escaped her notice, as it has before. She doesn't know if her forgetting is deliberate, or some kind of fateful favor. She knows it takes effort for her mother to call attention to it, as much as she would protest the notion. But she's a new age today, stamped by a new number. She makes herself a cup of tea and repeats the words, *birthday, birthday, birthday* in her head while running her fingers lazily along the wall. She says the words silently to the point that they are only sounds, *Birthday. Berth dae. Burthdais.* The sounds stretch unuttered between her tongue and palate, still numb from last night's soup. She lifts the tea to her face and lets the steam rise, clearing her sinuses, filling her head with clouds of hot oolong.

Later, while Iris is getting dressed, while the sun begins its downward creep, the phone rings again, her cell this time.

"Happy Birthday!" Mallory says. "We're going out. Please put on something fantastic and await further instructions." She hangs up with a menacing cackle before Iris can respond. This is a long-standing tradition between them. Since Mallory pried the date out of her when they were well into their junior year of college, she's made it her mission to make a big deal out of Iris's birthday. Iris is touched enough not to argue, though she does her best to let the big deal happen around or adjacent to, rather than about her. She tries to reciprocate in kind on Mallory's birthday. It's the only time she ever bakes.

She ambles back to the bedroom and looks in the mirror at the black T-shirt and khaki shorts she has put on. Her wet hair hangs down onto her shoulders, the tips darkening her shirt to a blacker black. She looks at her open closet, taking it all in as a sloppy color spectrum, clothes blending together, new and old, clean and dirty. The radio sings "96 Tears."

Digging through the back end of her wardrobe, Iris comes across a glittering gold cocktail dress that she bought at a yard sale because it was a dollar. She has never worn it, but a sense of reckless whimsy and the word *fantastic* in her head lead her to pull it out from the tangle. It smells of something stale, and feels filmy between her fingers. It feels as though she could just pull it apart. It would just stretch and separate like fly paper. She pulls off her clothes and steps into it, fastening it with a hook at the back of her neck. Goosebumps rise all the way down her bare back, a breeze of indeterminate origin.

She stands in front of the mirror and she is not herself. She is someone who wears gold cocktail dresses. Her first impulse is to take it off, but there is a shadow she casts. Against the bedroom wall, with the sun looming pink through the window, she sees her silhouette towering over the room. From where she stands, gold sequins send tiny rays of light through the air. She hypnotizes herself, and for a brief second wonders what makes a self, maybe a self is as mutable as a half breeze through a crack between the window and frame, the waning light, or a passing thought, with no substance to it at all. She blows her hair dry, puts on heels, fills a clutch with lipstick, keys, credit card, cell phone, and a twenty dollar bill folded into thirds. The phone rings again, and she is out the door.

Iris approaches the back railing of the brewery's patio. Though the lowering sun still hovers, and the air is mild, the restaurant has set its outdoor heat lamps to inferno. Mallory, leaning against the railing, sees her and waves her over. "Look at you," she mouths across the patio.

"I feel underdressed now," she says as Iris meets her. She is wearing a standard little black dress and suede boots that fold languorously around her ankles.

"It's dumb, right? This is a dumb dress."

"Shut up, it's your birthday. Nothing's dumb. Come with me." She takes Iris by the elbow and leads her through the front doors and into the restaurant. The music is loud, but impossible to hear.

Mallory yells, "Do you remember Nathan?"

"The one with the long hair? And the beard?"

"He shaved and cut his hair. He's actually cute now. We've been hanging out. Anyway, he and his friend Marcus are waiting for us at the table."

"Oh god. I didn't approve this." Iris's shoulders drop.

"And you never would have, which is why I am forced to lie to you all the time and never feel guilty about it."

They arrive at the table, where two clean-cut young men smile up at them expectantly. They wear the young guy kind-of-nice-but-not-*nice*-nice going out uniform of jeans and button down shirts. Iris wishes she had worn something different. There is too much air all over her.

In short order, they are sipping tall beers and Mallory is

engaged in intimate conversation with Nathan. She cannot hear what they are saying over the music, so she stops trying to listen.

"So," Marcus asks, "how old are you, anyway?"

"Isn't that one of those questions you're not supposed to ask, like how much money do you make?" She says this facing the tabletop, digging her nail into the grooves of *KISS Army*, which someone has carved in ballpoint pen, lord knows when.

"I don't know," he laughs, "I was just curious. Isn't aging the point of birthdays?"

"Twenty-five," she answers, looking up, a little bit charmed.

"I love your hair," he says.

"Oh, um, thanks."

Then he reaches a hand out to touch it and she flinches, but not enough to actually move her body.

"It's so soft I could run barefoot through it," he continues, working his fingers through. He hits a snag.

"Let me get that," he laughs, tugging at her hair.

"Ow!"

"Wait, wait, almost got it— there!" He frees his fingers and gives her hair one last stroke. Iris stares at the grain of the wooden table.

"You okay?" he asks. "Was that too forward? I'm sorry. I'm an idiot." He laughs nervously, but she doesn't look up.

"No— it's okay." She looks across the table at Mallory, whose eyes are closed, Nathan whispering something in her ear.

"Excuse me," Iris says, standing up, and Marcus squints his eyes shut and massages the bridge of his nose.

She makes her way through the brewery to the narrow hallway that houses the restrooms, tugging at her dress the whole way. The overhead lights, the walls, and the carpet are all different shades of red. She feels squeezed, lit, heated. She presses herself into a corner and dials her brother.

"Hello?"

"Hi."

A long pause follows, and Iris thinks she hears traffic.

"It's your birthday," Neil blurts out, breaking the silence.

"Yeah."

"I didn't forget."

"It's okay. You're allowed."

"I can hardly hear you. Where are you?"

"Out. Being the birthday girl."

"Good. That's what you should be doing. Right?"

"I know... I just can't relax."

"Sure you can."

"Do you?"

"What do you mean?"

"I know you have to be all bright and chatty for your job and all, but, do you feel that way for real? Do you usually... feel like you know exactly what's going on? Like that's really how you feel?"

"What?"

Iris pauses and tries to figure out how to re-arrange her thoughts so they make sense. "I just wish I knew how you do it."

"I don't know what you're asking me."

Iris peeks out at the bar and sees Mallory greeting more people she vaguely recognizes.

"But, you do," she says quietly.

"What?"

"But you do know," she says, a little louder now.

Neil doesn't respond.

"Hello?" she says. "Hello, are you there?"

Suddenly Neil is back on the line, with the fuzzy sound of the road amplified.

"Hello?" he says. "Hellllooooooooo?"

"I can hear you," she says, "I'm right here."

"Hello? Hello? Goddamnit," he says, and hangs up.

"Okay, um, I'll try back later," she mutters, and hangs up too.

She slips the phone back into her purse, but stays pressed to the wall.

Around her, the hallway still pulses red. She steps back out into the bar, where all she hears is bass. Whatever song is playing is lost in the belly-deep thump at the bottom of everything. The room is so dark, she can barely make out her table in the distance, where Mallory is now whispering in Nathan's ear, and Marcus is wiping up a spill with a wad of paper napkins, the new arrivals waiting at the bar for drinks. She looks up at the clusters of colored lights hooked to the ceiling's wooden beams. Up there they glow, white, orange, and blue. But the lights don't make it down to the floor. Nothing makes it all the way down to where she can reach it. She strains to make out any one sound amid the swirl of voices, the bass, and the clanking of glasses. It all blends together into a grinding whir, and she stands there, alone, camouflaged by the crowd, and remembers her seventh birthday, the one she spent locked in a shed in the backyard, listening to an old radio she'd found there, because she was too shy to be out among the other kids. She'd only meant to escape for a few minutes, to be alone with the music and the radio waves that she imagined she could see bouncing incessantly across the atmosphere, snaking around her in streams of electric blue, but then she heard the loud crack from the yard, and the waves stopped moving. The air stopped short, and hung in place.

She shakes it off, and re-focuses on the room she's in right now, the thump of the music, and how early it still is. She slides back into her seat at the table and takes note of the firmness of the wood beneath her, of the chill in this pocket of the room. She takes the last sip of her beer and rolls it around in her mouth, a little warm now, yeasty, and with a hint of orange. She squeezes the empty glass in her hand.

"I came back," she says into Marcus's ear, smelling his hair gel, and he gives her a half-smile.

Mallory pushes a shot across the table.

"Drink this."

"What is it?"

"No questions."

Iris eyes the brownish liquid in the glass, sniffs it, and pours it down her throat, bracing herself for the whiskey burn.

The boys at the table cheer and Iris feels nauseous. She asks Mallory for a cigarette and excuses herself to the patio. Mallory gives Marcus a little kick under the table, and he gets up and squeezes his way up to the bar.

Iris finds an empty nook against the patio railing and finds a candle to light her cigarette. Several feet from her, a couple is fighting, and Iris listens without looking up at them.

"No, *you* listen," the woman says, "I didn't come here to be humiliated."

"I don't know how the fuck I'm supposed to please you when I don't even know what the fuck you're talking about," the man pleads.

"Shut up," she hisses, and he does. Iris listens for a break in their silence, and glances casually in their direction, but they're lost in the crowd now. They could be anyone she sees, talking about anything.

"Hey," Marcus says, coming up behind her, and Iris spins around to face him, startled.

"Hi."

"Do you have another?" He indicates her cigarette.

"Oh, no— I got this one from Mallory."

"Ah, okay."

They stand facing each other for a moment, neither one thinking of anything to say to the other.

"Could I get a drag of that one?"

She passes him the cigarette, and he takes a quick puff before passing it back.

"You don't like going out much, do you?" he asks.

Iris looks back at him. "I guess it's… a little loud."

"But it's your birthday," he says brightly, and it sounds ridiculous to her, a sentence without meaning.

She opens her mouth to give some kind of answer, but she's struck by a sudden image of the view from the shed's dirty window, where she'd looked to see if the great crack from the yard had stopped the air outside the shed too. She'd stood on her toes, and peeked out to see her father drop a stack of paper plates onto the grass and take off running toward the crowd circled around the base of the fig tree. She saw her mother racing over from the driveway, dropping a paper grocery sack in the dirt and pushing through to the center, bodies parting to make way for the two of them, Sebastian howling in their wake. She remembers ducking then, and staying crouched there for a moment, face pressed to the dark wood. When she looked up again, she watched her brother climb down the tree, all eyes following him until the other mother, who must have been alerted somehow in her house just at the end of the road, whose wild eyes telegraphed the severity of what she saw before her, came rushing through, collapsing in a heap over her boy's limp body. After that, she didn't see anyone's face. All she saw were backs and profiles. All she heard was the wail of the ambulance, and the long silence that followed.

Iris puts the cigarette out in a glass ashtray and looks down at the patio's wooden floor, scuffed almost to a shine. She looks up at Marcus again, and he seems closer than before, though she can't say for sure. She hasn't been looking at his face, but in his general direction, taking in only the shape and general color of him, the pattern of his shirt. He picks up a glass of red wine from the table beside them and holds it out to her.

"Are you giving me some stranger's wine?"

"No, god— I set it down there. I don't know why I didn't give it to you right away. Sorry."

She takes a sip, and it coats her mouth in warmth.

"You should be happy," he says quietly, and Iris looks away.

Iris feels a growing chill against her arms then, and looks up to find the nearest heat lamp extinguished.

"I'm gonna go inside," she says, "it's kind of cold."

He nods, and Iris approaches the back door with him following a few feet behind.

She quickens her pace, bypassing the table and making a beeline for the ladies' room. She closes herself up in the stall farthest from the entrance and stands there, leaning her forehead against the door. Her fingers graze the hem of her dress, and she feels a rush of embarrassment at its shortness, its gaudy shine. She feels like a mouse trapped in the body of a flamingo. Then she remembers stepping out of the shed that night, into the dark, with no clue as to how late it was. The yard was empty, and in the distance, she could see the kitchen windows lit. She walked up to the tree and looked around. She saw the snapped branch on the other side and crouched down to touch its smooth, silvery bark, until her mother's voice came calling from the house.

"Iris, are you ready to come inside? Come here!"

She looked back, still crouched.

"Iris, get away from there, please!"

She looked back at the house, frozen in place, in her folds of bright yellow chiffon, neon in the colorless night, the sash untied and dragging in the dirt. She gripped the cold, loamy branch in her small hand and wondered, where could he be now? She'd seen the boy earlier, poking around near the shed, and she'd wondered if he could hear the music, if he would open the door and find her hiding place. Where did they take him?

"Iris, please!"

And the desperation in her mother's voice snapped her out of her trance. She walked slowly up to the kitchen door and her mother pulled her sharply inside by the arm.

"Change out of that honey," she said.

"Iris?"

Iris opens her eyes in the bathroom stall, collects herself, and steps out.

"Jesus," Mallory says, "I thought you'd passed out or something."

"I've got to get out of here..." Iris says, stepping out of the stall, realizing all at once that she's drunk.

"Seriously?" Mallory pouts.

"How are you getting home?" she calls after her, but Iris has already left the bathroom, the door swinging behind her.

She sees Marcus hovering near the bar and grabs his arm.

"Can you take me home? Now? It's too far to walk back in these shoes and I—"

"Yeah, yeah, sure," he says, and follows her out the door, nodding at his friend on the way out. When he gets outside, Iris is marching lopsidedly in the wrong direction. He takes her elbow and steers her toward his car.

When they pull up to Iris's building, Marcus turns off the ignition.

"So, this is you," he says, and brushes a finger down her forearm.

He lingers there, and Iris, sobered a little by the ride, can feel him inching closer. She's unwittingly sent a signal, she figures, and isn't sure whether or not she wants to take it back. He brings his face in to hers, and though startled, Iris lets him kiss her for a second. She keeps her eyes open, taking in his pores, the boyish peach fuzz on his upper cheek, and breathing in his thick, vaguely sweaty, but not unpleasant, scent. He slowly eases his tongue into her mouth, and she closes her eyes, and wonders how far this might go if she lets it. Her skin buzzes with the proximity and she surrenders to it, unnerved by the electricity that seems to be running through her. Then, abruptly, he pulls away.

"Okay, sorry," he says. "You're not into this. I get it."

"Oh. Oh." She doesn't know what she did.

"It's okay." He looks straight ahead, his cheeks flushed, hands on the steering wheel.

"Sorry," she says, and gets out of the car. As she's unlocking the front door, she looks back to find him still there, phone pressed to his cheek.

When she gets inside, she pauses on the stairs to her apartment for a moment, then turns back down toward the garage instead. She walks to her car, the clacking of her high heels echoing on the greasy pavement, lets herself into the passenger side and plunks herself down, feeling the exhaustion of standing on stilts all night. She opens up the glove compartment and pulls out the note.

It is later, and I'm not here. But you are.

She reads it several times. She leans her head back on the seat and closes her eyes, drowsy, heavy.

She drifts back to the kitchen doorway then, her mother's hand yanking her inside.

Change out of that honey, please.

She nodded, and walked down the darkened hallway, running her fingers along the wall. She stopped then, when she saw her brother's bedroom door standing open. She moved toward it and stepped inside, but he was nowhere to be found. The only thing she saw was the open window, and the curtains stirring in the breeze.

In her car, Iris opens her eyes and reads the note in her hand again.

I'm not here. But you are.

How would he know? How would she? She tucks the note

into her clutch and steps out of the car. She climbs the stairs up to her apartment, trying to feel the presence of her body in the air, but all she feels is the hang of her dress, as though there were no body inside it.

Drive

Neil yanks the Bluetooth out of his ear and throws it onto the backseat, thankful for the static that ended the conversation with his sister. These conversations always go the same way with Iris. She's sad or guilty or unsettled about something and will never say what it is. She expects him to say it for her. He stopped going to therapy at sixteen because he was sick to death of talking about it, of being probed for more feelings he wasn't sure he had. But Iris was spared all of that because she didn't see it, wasn't really there. Their parents figured she couldn't have been damaged like he must have been. They weren't scared for her. Of her. They left her be.

Driving home, it strikes him that he is always driving, though rarely home, to his twenties-era cottage apartment, the coziness of the set-up wasted on him. This is the first time in three weeks. It's the reason why he can't have any pets, or plants, or a wife. They would wither from his neglect. *I meant it this way*, he thinks. *I choose this over and over again.* He drives because he likes to drive, the rumbling feel of the road rushing beneath him like a current.

The freeway stretches out before him, free of traffic. He can go as fast as he wants. He tries to quell his growing aggravation at Iris. He feels his foot pressing harder on the accelerator and eases up. It's not her fault. But he tightens his grip on the steering wheel. He can't help it.

He's pared his memory of the accident down over the years,

cut out the preceding afternoon, cut out the scavenger hunt and the other kids running like clumsy hooligans through the yard, and his mom asking him to keep an eye on things while she went to get more ice cream, and he's cut out his father going to look for Iris who had wandered off again, who was always disappearing in plain sight, and he's cut out the boy's sharp animal cry as the branch finally snapped, the long moment as his small body hurtled against the lower branches, and the circle that formed around the tree, and the silence that consumed the place like nightfall and most of all he's cut out the weeks that followed, the watching eyes, the constant whispers, so that the whole drawn-out nightmare is signified by one thing, the worst thing, the only part that bears remembering: the hollowness in the boy's face when Neil looked down from his branch, cradling his own scratched and splintered hand, seeing, instantly, even from that height, that there was no one in there anymore. And then the crowd appeared.

But he hasn't really cut any of those things out. He just tells himself he has. The only part he can't and could never recall is how long he was up in the tree before he noticed the growing strain at the base of the branch the other boy was sitting on, and what moved him to climb up there in the first place, no matter how many times or how pointedly he was asked.

Briefly, he flashes back to his last session with the therapist. He was sitting on the dark green velveteen couch, looking down at the parking lot. It had been raining on and off all day, and the pavement was slick and glittering. He had an urge to slide his hands along its surface.

"Is there anything you want to talk about today, Neil?" the therapist asked, and Neil shook his head. Was this the only qualification necessary to become a therapist? Asking people how it's going? It seemed suddenly so absurd, that his mother would drive him twenty, thirty, forty miles outside of town— sticking with the same doctor, though they could never settle on a home for long— just to talk to this guy in a pilling argyle sweater who barely ever said anything. And since Neil barely ever said anything either, the hour passed slowly, he occasionally looking away from the window and back to the therapist, who was always already looking at him. Finally, he spoke: "So… what's the point of all this?" he said. "What do I have to do?"

"You don't have to do anything, Neil," he said, just barely smiling in the exact same way he always smiled, tilting his head as if to say, 'hey, come on, you know I get you, right?' which of course wasn't true.

Neil turned back to the window.

"So, I don't have to stay here, then?"

"It's absolutely up to you, always has been."

So he looked back to the therapist, stood up, and slowly crossed the room, expecting at any moment to be stopped, for the therapist to say, 'now hang on, we still have a lot of ground to cover.' Or, 'of course I meant that in a figurative sense.' But he didn't say anything. It was like he was giving his blessing, somehow, and Neil maintained tenuous eye contact with him as he opened the office door and stepped out sideways.

For the next forty-five minutes, he wandered the medical building, reading through lists of names on directories, riding the elevators up and down, and then out to the parking lot, where he dragged his fingertips against the wet backs of cars, taking his place at the building's entrance just before his mother pulled up in the station wagon with Iris asleep in the backseat. He climbed into the front seat without a word.

"Same time next week?" she asked, looking out the windshield in her caramel-colored sunglasses as she made a circle around the lot to get out.

He nodded, and in the backseat, Iris tossed and muttered in her sleep, her torso tangled up in the seatbelt.

He exits the freeway, but thinks briefly, as he always does, that he doesn't have to go home. He could keep going. No one

PART II

Roadblock

Iris walks up the stairs to the office, but she hits a roadblock at the landing between the two flights: a baby grand piano. Four men are trying unsuccessfully to carry it up. One man, in canvas overalls and a backward baseball cap, is wedged in between the piano and the wall. They push and grunt, but the piano is stuck; the man is stuck too. Iris stands below them and stares.

Suddenly, the man nearest to her turns his head and calls over his shoulder.

"Why the hell is there no service elevator in this building?"

"I don't know. Sorry."

"It's not your fault— didn't mean to snap."

"Motherfucker," the stuck man stage-whispers.

"Okay," the first man says, "everybody, very slowly, set it down."

Gently, they crouch down, letting the piano rest at an angle, half on the landing and half on the top flight of stairs. The men breathe heavily. The stuck man removes his hat and tosses it up the stairs. His thinning brown hair is pasted to his forehead.

"Who needs a piano so bad?" another of the four men says, rubbing his face with one hand, the other still clutching the bottom edge of the piano.

Iris wonders how she will get up the stairs. There is no other way up, unless she is willing to go outside and enter the hair salon next door, climb the stairs to their roof if they have stairs to their roof, leap across to her roof, and hope that she can get in some way. And hope that she can make the leap in the first place. She doesn't move.

The man who spoke to her digs through his pockets.

"Who has the delivery slip? I need the suite number."

One of the other men finds a folded piece of yellow paper in his pocket and hands it to the first man, the apparent leader, who reads aloud.

"Okay... 1137 Hearst Place... Suite 2B. Would someone go knock on their door?"

The stuck man makes a helpless face, twisting his stuck torso behind the piano. One of the unstuck men takes a step away from the piano as if to continue up the stairs.

"I'll go," Iris says sharply. He stops.

"How are you going to get up there?"

"I'll go," she says again, lowering herself to her knees.

The men watch as she flattens her torso against the lavender carpet, brushing against it, close enough to smell the no smell of it as she crawls underneath the piano. She inches forward, letting the carpet burn her bare elbows and knees, and stops when she is completely enclosed between the four legs, the naked wood dangling splinters above her head.

She looks up at it. The wood is so bare, untouched by the black lacquer that coats all visible sides. She shakes her purse off of her shoulder and begins digging through it, contained as she is in piano-shaped shadow.

"Are you stuck?" someone asks.

She pulls her Sharpie out and uncaps it with her teeth.

On the naked wood, she writes, *You won't even know I'm here.*

She zips the marker back into her purse and continues up the stairs. The light of the hallway feels warm against her skin, and like a lizard climbing a rock, she emerges from beneath the piano and rises to her feet.

She is poised to knock on the door of 2B when it opens, and

the man inside comes out and marches past her, the rush of air between them causing her head to turn and her eyes to follow him toward the stairwell. Her body follows her eyes.

"Is this your piano?" one of the delivery men asks.

"Yeah, yeah, bring it on up, I'm in 2B."

Iris stands behind him, facing the deliverymen. She makes a get-a-load-of-this-guy face at the stuck man, who returns her gaze with a what-are-you-gonna-do head shake. She swallows a laugh. She gasps it down her throat, mouth closed, and it works itself into a knot in her chest.

"Well, sir, we seem to have a problem," the leader says, motioning toward the piano with both hands.

The man from 2B squints.

"Oh. Oh, okay." He turns and disappears down the hallway and into his office. Iris has a notion to go to her office, but her boss is not around. She thinks he is supposed to be in Madrid this week, or... Malta? She only remembers the letter *M*. In any case, he is gone. It's early yet. She has some time to spare. They all blink at each other.

The man returns with a sledgehammer.

"Whoa whoa whoa," the leader says, hands up.

"Don't worry," he says, swinging the hammer slowly through the air like a batter cooling his heels at the plate.

The stuck man presses himself backward, creating a seal between his body and the wall. He swallows.

Iris watches from behind as the sledgehammer careens heavily into the stairwell, slowly at first, a test hit, sending plaster dust crumbling to the carpet. A few heads poke out of doors at the other end of the hall, but no one comes out. They are frozen in fear or confusion, or some mix of the two. Instantly, he swings it again, closer to the stuck man who tries to duck but is only able to bend slightly sideways and cover his head.

"What the fuck!" he yells into his arms.

"Don't worry." He swings again and again, building speed

until he settles on a rhythm. The noise of each hit echoes into the next, and a ropy vein pulses in the man's hairy forearm. Iris sees all his veins working overtime, purple and engorged. It occurs to her that he may not be able to stop as the wall begins to curve jaggedly inward. He has made his mark, but he keeps going.

Finally, he stops swinging. His arm hangs slack, weighted by the hammer.

"Okay, try now," he breathes heavily, wiping his forehead with the other hand.

Iris stares at his back, his white shirt damp and clinging. The men stare at the new wall.

"I am not going to be held responsible for this bullshit! There are forms you've gotta fill out, because this is not my responsibility," the lead deliveryman says, waving his arms toward the wall. More slowly, as though to a child, he repeats, "I am not. Responsible. For this." He pauses, his breathing steadying. "And I want that in writing signed by you."

"I know. Try it now."

The leader turns to look behind him, then looks back up the stairs. The man smiles, open faced, above them, the sledgehammer dangling at his side.

The four men grip the underside of the piano again, the stuck man now able to move through the hollowed out space. Together, they tilt it around the bend at the landing and up the second flight of stairs. Iris backs up against the opposite wall to let them past as they continue down the hall to 2B, the man trailing behind them, holding the hammer with both hands behind his back.

"How are you going to get it through the door?" she asks.

He stops and turns.

"What?"

"How are you going to fit the piano through your door?"

He turns back without answering her. Just then, the men stop. They set the piano down in the hall.

A voice calls out, "Sir?"

He flits down the hall and meets them in front of his door. Iris follows at a reasonable distance.

"What if you tilt it sideways?"

"No way."

"But I measured. It should fit."

"Well it looks like you measured wrong."

They continue back and forth, even at one point attempting a sideways tilt to appease him, but the legs are too long, and don't appear to detach. For a minute, they all stare at it glumly.

"I could make the doorway bigger."

"No," the formerly stuck man says emphatically.

Finally, a delivery slip is signed and the delivery men shuffle out, nodding to her as they pass. The man stands before his brand new piano and despondently taps middle C.

Iris begins to approach, but as she gets close, she hears the phone ringing in her office and feels compelled to answer it. He doesn't look up as she squeezes past the piano and lets herself in. She disengages the braying alarm as quickly as possible and pounces on the ringing phone.

"This is Larmax, Inc., how may I help you?"

"What time is it?" her boss asks, yelling into the phone over the sounds of traffic.

"I— I don't know!" she yells to match him. "I haven't turned my computer on yet." She presses the power button.

"It's not nine. Go home and then come back at nine."

"Where are you?"

"I'm in Milan. Until the end of the week. I have to go." He hangs up.

Iris watches her computer screen come to life and glances at the time. It is 8:47.

When she pokes her head back out, the man is gone. The

piano still sits in the corner between their two doors. She steps out into the hall.

There is no bench, so Iris stands while she runs her fingers lightly over the keys, too lightly, even, to make a sound. She drapes both hands over the keys and begins gently tapping her fingers against them, letting them dance across in silence. She never did learn to play piano. This way, she can play anything and it will sound beautiful.

She closes her eyes and listens to the sound of her fingers slipping on the ivory, slowly, across and back, until the door to 2B opens with a swift thud and she instinctively jerks her hands behind her back.

The man does not look at her as he steps out and unfolds a padded nylon slipcover, which he spreads across the piano, pulling it this way and that so it hangs evenly. Iris watches, curling her toes inside her shoes.

"What are you going to do with it?" she blurts out.

"Huh?" he says, smoothing a wrinkle.

"I was just wondering what it's for."

He stops adjusting the slipcover and stands up to face her.

"I'm not sure that I'm sure yet," he says. "But it seemed like a nice, heavy thing to have."

"Aren't you worried," she asks, "that someone might complain… you know, about the wall? About you?"

He looks down at the piano again and rubs his hand in a slow circle over the slipcover.

"I don't really think anyone will bother to complain," he replies, "do you?" He looks up then and watches her unmoving face for a moment. She feels his eyes searching, imagines them like small rays of light trawling across her skin, but she can't bring herself to meet his gaze before he turns around and steps back inside.

She doesn't know who would complain. She doesn't, in fact, know to whom one would complain. It's not as though there's anybody in charge here.

Sounds of Sleep

The home office always feels strange to Neil, like a neglected great-aunt's house— a burden, a source of disquieting and inexplicable guilt. Not one solitary thing about the place has changed in the years he's spent in Shaffer-Bruns' employ, not the color of the walls, not the smell of the elevator, not the position of one single chair. Only the people have changed, the original Shaffer and Bruns having been replaced by a series of go-getters and benefactors of nepotism, bodies and hair slid into the same suits, the receptionist a vaguely different brunette every other month. His stomach flutters, his head pulsing. He only just flew back.

No, he remembers, it's been a couple days. So why does he still feel like a foggy approximation of himself? Why does that tightness, that dryness in his blood stay with him?

Neil realizes he hasn't been listening to the pitch, and straightens his posture, as though it signifies his investment in the meeting.

"What we have here," Mason continues, "is a revolution in personal regeneration— more commonly known as sleep. But what we're looking to do with this product is sell the idea of living up to one's full potential. The idea of perfectly restful sleep as the key to personal betterment and success— not just a product, but an idea of what never was, but now might be."

He listens, kind of. Mostly he is just sick, and thinking about the sickness. The place has obviously been cleaned within the last couple hours, because the scent of industrial-strength cleaning fluid burns his nostrils, but the place still looks dirty. A plastic plant sits next to him, its leaves covered in a thin layer of dust, his first clue it's a fake. All these conference rooms are the same, he thinks. You can't clean them enough— they always seem to be hiding something— why else would they need to be cleaned with goddamn pine-scented lighter fluid every day. His nausea is still in check, though, probably.

His attention drifts as his colleagues strategize, and he remembers lying in bed in the summertime as a kid, with the mosquitoes buzzing outside his window, how he'd kick off the sheets and revel in his nakedness, with just those hints of light coming through the blinds like lasers, that cumulative yellow glow. He would lie like that, feeling that he was waiting for something. But what age is he imagining himself to be. Six? Thirteen? And where— what window, what bed? He feels no physical connection to any of his former bodies.

"What does everyone want?" Mason pauses two seconds, one, two, before answering his own question, "to be his or her best self. To be free from the worry that he or she is languishing, squandering his or her time on earth. We have to get to the heart of these desires— which are also fears, can't forget that."

Listening now, quietly flustered, Neil wonders if he missed the introduction of the product, the actual physical object he's to be selling. He makes eye contact with Mason and juts his chin upward.

"Finch?"

"Yeah, I'm sorry, did I— what is this again?"

His colleagues exchange looks.

"We went over this at the beginning. It's a sleep aid."

"Okay, sorry. You mean, like, a pill?"

Mason puts down his laser pointer, sending the red light ricocheting across the table and against the opposite wall.

"Okay, let's skip forward briefly so you can all get a feel for the product and then we'll continue from there. Angela, could you bring in the samples?"

Mason's assistant rises from the table and returns a minute later with a cardboard box, from which she distributes a collection of cellophane packages containing fluffy fabric eye masks with small speakers by both ears. Neil opens his and straps it onto his face with a Velcro strip in the back.

"Now press the button just above your right ear. No, your right. Okay, everybody got it? Okay, I've got mine on too now. Now what do you notice?"

Neil presses his button, and hears a gentle lap of water, a mild, slow wind, and then a sound he can't identify, some kind of ambient, warped sound, like some inarticulate, anguished call.

"I hear crickets," a new saleswoman says.

"I could fall asleep right here, no joke," says another guy, "this is awesome."

"I... uh... I'm not sure what this is supposed to be," says Neil.

"I think you've got whale songs," says Mason, "but more importantly, how does it make you feel?"

Neil pictures the room then, all of them facing each other around the big oblong conference room table, blindfolded.

"Um... good, I guess?" He listens to the plaintive wail, seemingly so far away, but really nestled right by his ear, and imagines himself marooned in a paddleboat on some murky sea. The room disappears for him, and he feels suddenly, palpably trapped.

"Good. Now keep these on for now, and let's talk about where we go from 'good'."

THIEF

At noon, Iris goes to the café for lunch. She orders a tuna salad sandwich and selects a table on the patio, right next to the wooden railing. Behind it: a thick row of greenery, then the sidewalk, then the street. She sits facing out to watch traffic, but the cars are blending together today. She is unable to latch onto their drivers, to focus on their faces long enough to imagine identities and destinations for them. They may as well be running independently, a thousand driverless cars careening toward the freeway onramp. She takes a bite of her sandwich, the bread toasted a deep brown, the filling too dry.

She has brought nothing to read. She reads the words, "Mike sucks" carved into the white metal table and wonders what Mike did and maybe he deserves this character assassination and maybe he doesn't, but whoever wrote it wins or thinks they have won, she supposes.

A horn honks and jolts her out of her reverie, but all she sees is a blonde woman in her fifties parallel parking between two empty cars, no one else around, and she honks again, mad in general.

Iris turns her gaze away from the street and toward the planter that runs all the way along the railing, assorted greenery tangled together, a smattering of flowers. She tries to describe this view to someone in her head. *It was beautiful*, she begins to someone, not meaning it, starting something not worth finishing. She doesn't know the names of any of these plants, any of these flowers, and she can't tell where they begin or end, or who planted them, or when they will die. All these planned pockets of nature are indecipherable to her. It's all just spilling yet contained. She squints against the sun and feels a headache rising from the base of her skull. She's lost her appetite.

A hoarse laugh comes roiling from two tables down, and she turns to look, shielding her eyes from the sun with her hand. The old men are both laughing now. She didn't even see them. They clutch their knees and lean backward into their laughter, crumb-filled plates and empty glasses piled between them. The laughter sounds painful, as though forced out with the last of their air. She didn't hear the joke.

When Iris gets back to the office, she notes the mangled wall at the top of the stairs, but the piano has disappeared from the hall. Airlifted, demolished, vaporized, plucked in the span of a lunch. She stands in the space it had previously occupied and leans forward to press her ear against the door of 2B, but the door is all she hears.

Inside her office, she quickly checks the window that looks down over the parking lot. The white van is gone, so the man must be gone too. But where did the piano go?

She drops her bag onto her desk and steps into the hall again. She stands for a moment, facing 2B's door, before trying the doorknob. It doesn't open at first, leading her to presume it's locked, but she jerks the knob hard one last time and it pops open with a scuffing sound, as though she's broken through something. Startled but not displeased, Iris steps inside.

Not much has changed, though the place seems neater, boxes tucked away somewhere. The only evidence of a Murphy bed is a skinny rectangular outline in the wall that she wouldn't even notice if she weren't looking for it. And for the first time, she notices another door, in the wall farthest from 2A and painted the same color so it blends in seamlessly, a closet maybe, or leading to a whole other room, but when she tries it, it won't open. Even when she shakes and pulls with all her strength, caring little whether she breaks the knob clean off, it won't open.

Finally she lets go and pulls her sweating hands away. She turns around then, catching her breath, and her gaze settles on a little radio, the little radio she's heard him play day after day, morning after morning, sitting on the windowsill. She picks it up and turns the dial a few times, each tick bringing her to a different quality of static, some crackling, some hissing, some barely audible at all.

She turns it off, and only then notices how dusty it is. She blows on it, and a cloud of dust disperses and floats down to the carpet. She clutches it to her chest, and before she quite takes note of what she's doing, she's left the room, closing the door behind her, stepping back inside her own office, and dropping the radio in her purse, glancing about with forced casualness, as though someone might be watching.

Before she leaves at the end of the day, she checks the window again, seeing that the white van has returned, in a different spot now. After setting the alarm and locking up, she stops at the door of 2B and nestles her face at its edge, where she can squint into that thin space that leads directly into the room. She narrows her eyes and imagines she can see him in there, or at least the rough shape of him, and that he can feel her on the other side of the door.

She thinks about knocking, but something stops her. She stands back, hanging there for a moment before backing away slowly, turning just as she reaches the top of the stairs.

Disasters

On the way home, she stops at the grocery store to pick up milk, cereal, lettuce, iced tea, and trash bags. She grips her penciled list against the steering wheel as she pulls into the parking lot, the sweat from her palm wilting the gas station receipt paper. Her palms sweat when she drives, just like her mother's do. As a child riding in the passenger seat, she watched her mother wipe her hands off on her jeans at every stop light. When she noticed Iris looking, her mother would laugh nervously and look away, every time. How much sweat on every trip downtown, to the store, to the dentist, over and over through the years, how many small laughs, how many sheepish looks between them have been exchanged and forgotten? On longer trips, it was her father who always drove, her mother looking out the window, right temple pressed to the glass, her eyes turned to the road. Iris wipes her hands off under her seat and puts the car in park.

In the brightly fluorescent lit store, she picks a basket from the stack and starts down the bakery aisle to admire the decorated cakes before attending to her business. The lights, the expansive artificiality of them, make her feel like it is 3:00 in the morning, though the aisles are packed with workers on their way home. It makes her think of disasters, and of preparations for long car trips, driving toward safety, into the night.

Disaster is another word whose meaning is probably a little different from the meaning she ascribes to it. The word brings up images of blank faces and closed doors. She can't quite imagine what the beginning of a disaster would look like. She wonders, if she were ever in a position to witness one unfolding, if she were right there in the middle of it, would she recognize it?

She stops in front of the bakery case, cupcakes sitting in perfect rows of color and sheet cake decorated with gritty buttercream flowers, so close behind glass, she can just feel her finger running along the icing, digging down into the spongy center, finally burying her hand wrist-deep. The smell of the bakery aisle does something to her. The smell is right there. It resets her senses. She takes one more deep breath and joins the throngs.

In the cereal aisle, Iris picks up a box of raisin bran and places it in her basket. She idly glances off toward the produce section, wondering what else she might need, and her eyes stop at the teeming rows of melons. There, a man in a navy blue suit, a man just the right height, with just the same thinning reddish blond hair and verging on sickly-pale complexion, and just the same delicate profile as her boss is concentrating on cantaloupes, holding them up one by one and gently squeezing them, bringing them close to his face and breathing them in. He is so involved in what he is doing that Iris decides it is safe to take a closer look.

She takes a few steps forward, lining herself up with the condiment aisle, eye level with the Worcestershire sauce and spicy brown mustard. She closes her eyes for a moment and sniffs, but the smells are contained, bedlam if they were to mix. She imagines a grocery store with no packaging, with everything right there to touch and smell and hold and lick, tidal waves of spaghetti sauce and hills of crackers and chips and croutons to crunch in one's fists and her breath slows and maybe she is just hungry...

But it couldn't be him, could it? He's in Milan until the end of the week. That was today that he said that, wasn't it? She tries to put the days of the past week in order by what she was wearing, but then she can't remember what she wore the day before yesterday, and then the man who may or may not be her boss starts to walk away— no cantaloupe selected, not even carrying a basket— and she follows him at a safe distance, ducking behind a soda display when he turns slightly, and that is when she knows it is him. It is the look in his eyes, somehow both confident and confused, as he looks back at the produce section, as though he does not know why he came into the store in the first place, and he is certainly going to have a word with someone about it.

He walks out of the store and Iris stands up from behind the display. The grocery list seems to have fallen from her hands somewhere in the store and she can't remember everything else she needed, so she just gets milk, the raisin bran's natural companion, and checks out.

At home, she sets her purse and plastic grocery bag by the door and kicks off her shoes. She puts on a Buddy Holly CD and starts to run a shower, letting it run until it is scorching hot, then adding cold until it is just right. She steps out of her clothes, leaving a puddle of fabric on the bathroom floor and turns up the stereo. Buddy Holly sings *Rave on, it's a crazy feeling, and I know it's got me reeling*, and she steps in, letting the water rush over her head and down her face, and then the water is all she hears.

* * * *

Eighteen months ago, or twenty. It gets harder and harder for her to remember how long it's been, how many summers she's spent sweating in her car in polyester and tweed. One, two? She marks the time as one gives a toddler's age, but she stopped marking at some point. Those months ago, those days and days upon days and more days ago, it was just an ad in the classifieds. She had been fired from another waitressing job, this time for continuing to pour iced tea after the glass was already full just one too many times. She always apologized, but sorry doesn't get the stain out. It was their own fault for having those giant windows that looked out over a cliff. She would stare out, imagining that this was the edge of the earth, the spot where gravity petered out, that each time she stepped out the door at the end of her shift, she was taking the chance of drifting up and off. She couldn't keep her mind on the task at hand.

She didn't know what she should do instead, but something different seemed in order, something with less immediate potential for calamity.

Seeking receptionist for busy office. Must be self-starter, multi-tasker.

There was an address, and instructions to apply in person between 9:00 and 10:00 a.m. She wasn't sure what it meant to be a self-starter or a multi-tasker, but she had gone to college, hadn't she? She could probably do anything she was asked to do. She showed up at 9:15 the following morning dressed in a navy pencil skirt and white blouse, her one professional outfit. She pressed the button for suite 2A and announced herself. She waited, but there was no answer. She tried again. "Hello?" she said, holding down the button. "I'm here about the job?" But there was only the faint radio crackle.

So she stood on the steps until a FedEx deliveryman was buzzed in and she followed him inside. When she found 2A, she knocked. She waited. She opened the door and walked into a flurry of activity, people huddled together over computers, arguing, doors flying open and shut, the phones ringing ringing ringing. It seemed to her that she had never heard anything so loud. She turned and walked out, she hoped, before anyone noticed she was there.

She went back a couple of days later wearing the same outfit, again waited for someone to follow, again walked in when her knock went unanswered. This time, things were calmer, just a few people at desks typing in silence. Then one by one, their phones started ringing, until everyone was saying *hello how are you I'm great* all at once and the din of voices was too much and she started to walk back to the door when a voice distinguished itself from the others.

It was clear and strong, and it said, "Can I help you?"

Iris looked back and there he stood, a small, pale, reddish-blond-haired man in a suit. He had translucent gray eyes that looked right at her.

"I'm here about the receptionist job?" she asked.

"Ah, yes," he said. "Good good," and led her to his office.

Iris had never been in a professional setting like this. At least she had never gone past the lobby, into the guts of the place. A place. Since her dismissal from the Blackbird Diner, she had been coasting on her meager savings and postponing the inevitable until her time ran out and she was out of money, completely out, a balance of zero, satisfying almost, the flatline of it. As she followed him down the hallway, she glanced into each office decorated with fake plants and fake art and real families, tacked up in two dimensions on particleboard, everyone drinking coffee coffee and more coffee. *Why don't people drink lemonade or ice water*, she thought. *It's hot out.* Then the chill of the air conditioner penetrated her skin, and she understood that the weather didn't matter. In here, her body wouldn't know hot from cold or up from down either. When they got to his office, he sat behind his desk and directed her to the chair across from him. He pushed a few piles of papers aside so there was a clear space between them, where he rested his hands palms down for a moment before folding them.

She wondered if she was supposed to say something.

Seemingly sensing her discomfort, he nodded toward the mess of papers on his desk and smiled. "This is precisely why I need you. To rein me in."

Iris nodded, smiled with closed lips.

"You've answered phones, yes?"

"Yes," she nodded again. Her own phone. Her parents' phone.

"Good. Listen," he said, rising, "I need to be going now—we'll go over everything Monday."

She frowned, confused, but righted her expression quickly. She fumbled out of her chair and followed him out of his office, but he never looked back, and kept walking right out the main door.

Iris paused and looked around at all the desks. She didn't even know what they were doing, typing, talking. They didn't get that far. She had the job before she walked through the door. Even before she saw the ad, while she was lying in bed awake in the summer muck, wondering *how*, wondering *what*, she had it.

When she showed up for work the following Monday wearing the same outfit, as yet unable to afford another one, the layout of the suite had changed. Now there was only one desk in the lobby area, equipped with a computer and telephone. She sat down at it and waited. From time to time she heard a door open or close, or bits of conversation from other offices, but no one came out. She checked the boss's office, but he wasn't there.

When the phone on her desk rang, she picked it up.

"Larmax, Inc. Hello?" She looked around, hoping for someone, anyone to bail her out.

"Can I help you?"

The man on the other end asked to be connected to accounting.

"One moment, please," she said, and tucked the receiver into her desk's empty top drawer, trying in vain to place it gently, so the person on the other end wouldn't hear a thump or clatter.

She knocked on the first door she came to and walked in, panicked, before anyone responded. A woman looked up from her desk, annoyed.

"Excuse me?"

"I'm sorry," Iris said, "but who does someone talk to if they want to talk to accounting?"

The woman paused a few seconds. "Voicemail," she said.

Iris returned to her desk and figured out how to forward the call to voicemail, whose voicemail she didn't know. She decided then that this woman would be her go-to until the boss returned to fill her in on her duties. She wondered if she should go back and introduce herself. She felt like a trespasser, an unwelcome addition and she needed an ally.

A few minutes later, the boss arrived, disheveled, blaming traffic for his tardiness, and gave her a quick rundown of her tasks: Phones, faxes, errands. She wrote down everything he said, hungry for instruction.

He coached her on her inflection.

"When you answer, say, 'Larmax, Inc.' with an upward lilt. Not like it's a question, just... do you see what I'm saying? Just, inviting. Right?"

She practiced in the car on her way home, in the shower, again and again until it was perfect, a coo, automatic.

The next day, she looked for that woman, to thank her for helping her out on her first day, but she never saw her. Every time she checked her office, it was empty.

As the months wore on, the number of people in the office seemed to dwindle. At least seemed to. She didn't know what number they had started at. Over time, the number of sandwiches she fetched at lunchtime fell to five, then four, then the lunch orders stopped coming. She could park anywhere she wanted. The boss was frequently away, but there didn't seem to be anyone in charge in his absence. She never learned any names because she never seemed to see anyone more than once, or never for more than a minute or two at a time. She got so used to saying, *I'm sorry, he's not in right now, may I take a message?* that she sometimes said it even when he was there, right down the hall.

Some time later, he called from a business trip to tell her he wouldn't be in that day, or the next day, and that he wasn't going to tell her where he was so that she wouldn't have to lie if anyone asked.

"You'll just say you don't know. Okay?"

"Okay."

He hung up before it occurred to her to ask who he was avoiding, when they might call, or what she was to do in the meantime. She wouldn't have asked anyhow. As long as her phone kept ringing, as long as she had a to-do list, as long as she had a place to go every morning and enough money to keep herself alive, and as long as she didn't have to look directly at the earth's edge, then nothing else mattered.

* * * *

Iris blinks heavily and realizes she must have been in the shower a long time, because the water is freezing. The CD is back at the beginning, and Buddy Holly is singing about that crazy feeling again. She shuts off the water and rubs out the goosebumps on her arms.

She dries off and pads into the kitchen, where she sees that her grocery bag is still sitting by the door. She checks the milk and finds that it has gone lukewarm, so she pours it all down the drain, and she won't eat the raisin bran dry, so really, it is as though she hasn't run the errand at all. She wasn't even at the store. She didn't see anything.

Day Off

When he gets home, Neil drops his things in the kitchen and examines the contents of his fridge. He has an urge to cook something really elaborate and messy, like enchiladas suiza, and use every utensil and piece of cookware in the house, or something that would require a whole lot of chopping, like ratatouille. *Just really fucking COOK*, he thinks. But he doesn't have any real food, just a box of mac n' cheese and a mysterious Tupperware container he isn't about to open. And he's too tired to go to the store, and he'd resent his own whimsy when it came time to do the dishes anyhow, so he makes the mac n' cheese and leaves it to cool on the counter.

He steps over to the couch and lies down, kicking off his shoes and letting them drop off the side with a thud. He rolls over onto his stomach and shuts his eyes— just for a second, he thinks, his eyeballs dry and throbbing. Tomorrow is his first real day off in weeks. He tries to think about what he'll do with the time. He'll run some errands, sure, but then what? He pictures himself strolling through some park with coffee and the paper, but he doesn't know what park it's supposed to be. Has he even been to any parks in town? He can't even remember seeing any. He pictures himself going places, far away places, marching in step with the plump yellow sun, following its command as though he is the only one listening hard enough to hear it. His mind's eye is filled with the glow of this imaginary sun, and he sinks into it, into a heavy sleep, the phone in his front shirt pocket pressing itself into his chest.

POCKET

Iris decides to do laundry to clear her mind. If she focuses on a specific task, then she can forget that this day ever happened, and anything forgotten is not any *thing* at all. She throws clothes gathered on the bathroom floor into the hamper and hauls it all to the laundry room, detergent and jar full of quarters clutched to her chest.

She loads the laundry and sits on the floor watching her clothes swim like soapy anemones through the glass. The room is so warm and white that she loves to wait while the machines run, despite the multiple signs warning of toxic substances in the room. She can't imagine there could be anything so toxic here, and what does *toxic* even mean? She breathes in the smell of other people's soap and fabric softener, crumpled sheets of it haunting the corners of the room like dust.

When it is time to switch her clothes to the dryer, she finds that all three of them are filled with dry clothes that are cool to the touch. The clothes are a little stiff and musty, as though they've been sitting a long time. Someone has forgotten that they ever did laundry, or decided to simplify their life, right in the middle of a cycle, relinquishing material things once and for all. She could imagine herself doing the former, but not the latter. She pulls the clothes out of two dryers and stacks them on the folding table, loading her own in their place. It is always startling when she is reminded of the neighbors she sees so rarely. It is as though there is a silent understanding that no one will walk the halls at the same time. She feels awkward handling someone else's underwear and children's socks, so she goes back to her apartment after loading the quarters and pressing start.

She fills and fires up the tea kettle, and then hears her phone ringing from her purse. She lowers the flame of the stove before going to answer it; the screen tells her it's Neil.

"Hello?"

He doesn't say anything.

"Hello? Hello?"

Still nothing, and Iris sits down, listening as the silence takes the form of an underwater beat.

"Hello?" she tries one more time.

Then she turns up her phone's volume, so the beat is more distinct, and gradually, she begins to think she hears soft breathing.

He's asleep, she thinks, and covers the other ear so she can hear better.

It's been a while since he's pocket-dialed her. When it happens, she always stays on the line. Usually, she hears the rustling of his pocket, muffled voices, maybe the sound of a car door slamming. Now she turns in to face the couch cushions, and pictures Neil curled up like a cat beside her.

The beat she perceives sounds labored, somehow, as though it is coming up against resistance. It has force behind it, and she thinks the breathing sound is strained too. It strikes Iris how pitiful it might seem that she is clinging to this voyeurism as some proof of closeness, but she can't help but cling, knowing all too well how easily he can slip away. Shortly after the accident, before they packed up the house and moved away, he started going for walks after dinner, long walks that would have him gone until very late. Iris always wanted to follow him, but she restrained herself, sensing that he wanted to be alone. She would lie in bed and imagine him scaling mountains, finding caves in forests she imagined could be found beyond the limits of their small town.

When he kept doing it in their new town, their parents came to accept that he needed to go off by himself. His therapist told them it was perfectly normal. His therapist told them to let him have this one private thing. That's what Iris gleaned, at least, from listening in on her parents' side of the phone conversations, crouched outside an open window, hugging Sebastian's face to her hip with the mosquitoes buzzing.

Then one night, he didn't come back. In the morning, their parents were struck dumb with worry. This time, Iris thought to listen in on the phone in her parents' bedroom as her mother muttered unintelligibly to the police on the kitchen phone, her father standing back with arms crossed against the living room wall. The police told her to calm down. They took her name and told her they couldn't file a missing persons report this soon, and they asked her, *Finch, huh? Isn't your boy the same one who's always wandering at all hours?* Her mother hung up then, and Iris listened to the dial tone for a minute.

When Neil walked through the front door a couple of hours later and climbed the stairs to his bedroom, he didn't say a word to anyone. Their parents stood at the bottom of the stairs and watched him in silence, clutching their own hands. Iris was stepping out of the bathroom in her towel at the top of the stairs as he came up, and she was so startled to see him, as though she had already settled on the idea that he had run away for good, and she recalls now how un-startled he looked, how thoroughly aloof, as he walked past her into his room, and shut the door.

"Neil, can you hear me?"

The sounds seem to soften now, and she wonders if he was dreaming— like when a dog starts whimpering or kicking his legs in his sleep— or is dreaming still.

"Goodnight," she says, and hangs up, as the kettle begins its high, mournful whistle.

DISINTEGRATION

There on the pristine Ikea couch, with stocking feet hanging off one side and his mouth open against the upholstery, Neil dreams that he is swimming toward a buoy that bobs in the distance, in water so murky he feels his body disappear beneath its surface, his arms only re-materializing as they reach up to stroke. His muscles pulse powerfully, arcing forward, up into the cool air, but as soon as they dip back down into the water, he feels lost, helpless as a ghost, his kicks theoretical at best, bringing him no closer to anything, his body a cloud of particles pressing together and releasing in a never-ending cycle.

Somehow, he reaches shore, and then, somehow, a city, where an undefined cataclysmic event has occurred. He finds himself pulling bodies out of buildings, running from rushing fireballs, punch-kick-shoving his way through the wreckage. He's saving himself, and a growing pack of followers, out of the darkness.

When he finally wakes up, blinking fast and flicking his head from side to side until the realization of his body and couch dawns on him, he can't piece together what was happening. The only image he retains is of himself, running, running into nothing and away from everything, and that too begins to fade as he perches himself up on his elbows and glances, puffy-eyed, at the cold macaroni on the counter.

Signal

After folding and putting away the laundry, Iris gets ready for bed, and while she's wandering through the apartment brushing her teeth, she pulls the little radio out of her purse. It's so small and toy-like, a physical cartoon. She switches it on again and turns the dial slowly in search of a station, but still she finds only approximations— vague, formless music mostly drowned out by snow, quiet voices bulldozed by a steady crackle, and then nothing. She sets it down on the couch and returns to the bathroom.

In bed, Iris lies there, wanting sleep. And as the night grows darker outside her window, and sleep finally finds her, she sinks down again, into the place where her dreams have taken up residence.

In the old house, she finds herself in the overstuffed shed, the walls teeming with rusty tools, boxes for long-forgotten appliances, a pile, ceiling high, of *Time* magazines.

On the floor, next to an old, splintered yellow table, she finds a radio. It is not an old radio, but it has been forgotten. She runs her finger over the speakers and draws a line through the soft layer of dust. She leans down and blows, loosening a cloud of it. The dust settles all around, spread thin now, dissipated but not gone. She picks up the radio and cradles it in her arms, walks out the door into the house with the cord trailing on the ground.

She walks through the kitchen, where Sebastian still lazes on the kitchen table, past the picture window that looks out onto the yard. She hears voices coming from out there, frenzied little murmurings building in volume, but when she looks, there's nobody there, and the voices have stopped. For a moment, she stands still, waiting for them to start up again, but they don't. Sebastian follows her with his eyes as she continues down the hallway. In her room, with its flickering overhead lamp and shutters closed tight, she plugs the radio in between two heavy oak bookshelves and sets it on an empty shelf. The radio lights up. It's been waiting for this.

She turns the dial slowly, stopping at each station, though nothing is coming in. With each turn of the dial, the static grows more opaque, a wall of sound that creates a kind of hush throughout the room, objects becoming even more still. The house stops creaking. There is no space in the air anymore.

Finally, the dial hits on something. Clear as water, a signal comes in. Iris backs away from the radio and sits on the cold floor. She pushes her body in between the two bookshelves and hums along, humming, *You send me, darling you send me, honest you do, honest you do, honest you do*, and the trees outside bend beneath the solid force of the wind. Everything bends ever closer to the ground.

Tucked safely between the bookshelves with her eyes closed, Iris feels this happening, but when the song ends, another doesn't come on. There is no static, only silence. The room is filled again with the breath of objects, the imperceptible fidgeting of a stapler on the desk, of a sofa sinking on its springs.

She glances around her and is suddenly struck by the fact that this isn't her room. She gravitated toward it instinctively, but— there's no bed. There are none of her things. She doesn't even recognize this room. She rises quickly and opens the shutters to find the same yard she looked out at just minutes before, only the sun is brighter, as though it's moving in closer, illuminating and alienating her at once. She tries to open the window, but it's locked, and she can't find the latch.

On a hunch, she tries the door; it's locked too.

"Hello?" she says, then louder, "Hello!" and at that, she hears Sebastian run to the door and begin to snarl, his growling erupting finally into a persistent bark.

She retreats back to the window, and she can just barely hear the voices outside again, whispering, chattering, but from the small window, she can't see anybody, nor make out any words.

"Hello?" she tries again, toward the window this time, but the glass is thick, the sun full and blinding.

The sun isn't going anywhere, and neither is she, and suddenly, she wonders if the dog on the other side of the door is Sebastian at all, but then she is awake in her own bed in her own apartment and her fear feels misplaced. It is dissipated but not gone. She lies back on her pillow, crickets chirping outside her city window, and does not fall asleep again.

SICK

The night turns over into morning and Iris sits up in bed. She can tell already that it will be a hot day, as the sun shines mercilessly bright rays into her room. Then her alarm goes off and she hits it before the second beep. She blinks slowly and winces. Her eyes ache. The relief of closing them lasts only until they open again. It is as though she has no control over the operation.

She walks into the kitchen to dig around for breakfast. There, she sees the empty milk bottle on the counter, the unopened box of cereal turned on its side. Her hunger pulls at her, the distinction between nausea and want blurred. She tears the top off the box and begins shoveling the cereal into her mouth, barely swallowing before pushing the next handful in. The urgency of her hunger finally recedes and she sets the box down on the counter. She coughs and a slimy chunk of bran flies back up her throat and into her mouth. She spits it out into the sink.

She slumps over to the couch, the little radio sitting where she left it. She picks it up and begins to examine it, peering into its holes, blowing more dust out of it. She stares at it, its speakers like big insect eyes, its cassette deck mouth. If it was his, it's hers now, and though it fills her with a kind of satisfaction to have something of his, she isn't sure why she took it, or what she plans to do with it, if anything.

She sits there, still turning the radio over in her hands and goes over the day as she expects it to unfold. Traffic. Park. Up the stairs. Alarm. Desk. Phone. Light of the computer screen. She will listen for any movement from the man next door, and it will come or it won't. Or maybe it's her turn now, and she'll wait for any movement from herself. She will have messages or she will have a list of tasks and she will do them or she won't or she will spend twenty minutes in the sickly green-lit bathroom while women bang on the door and she will not be able to operate the doorknob.

"I'm sorry," she'll say. "I'm trying, I am." And when the banging grows more urgent, she'll search the walls frantically for a window that will never materialize.

She tries to picture the man next door in his office, doing whatever he is doing, but his features are hard to delineate. It's as though she's never quite looking at him. She's so intimidated by his presence that she can't bring her eyes to focus on him. She stares into the radio's face again, and tries to imagine his, but all she can conjure is his earthy smell, and the way he seems to fill space, even through a wall, in such a way that she can feel it in her own space. His face could be anybody's. Inertia keeps her sitting, keeps her staring at the radio in her hands. She turns it on, turns the dial a notch and snowy static fills the room. She switches it off again, and puts the radio down.

A thought occurs to her, then. She gets up and goes into the kitchen, quickly outlining a brief speech in her head, and reaches for the cordless phone on the wall.

She dials the office until her own voice greets her, *Thank you for calling…*

At her own voice's prompting, she dials 3 for her boss's voicemail and again she is greeted warmly, this time by the boss. Everyone is so polite when they're not there. At the tone, she gears herself up to sound pitiful.

"Hi," she says, "it's me. I am so sorry to do this, but I have an awful sore throat and a fever of a hundred and one. I don't think I'm going to be able to come in today. Hopefully, I'll be better tomorrow. Sorry."

She drops the phone on the counter and leans on her elbows. The new emptiness of the day looms ahead like a fog. She expects to feel guilty. She expects the guilt to envelop her, encase her limbs. But this isn't guilt. This is something else. This is something she could see herself doing more often.

She heads back to her bedroom and dresses in a pair of cut-offs and a white tank top, the sunlight pushing the walls of her small apartment inward. She combs knots out of her hair and wonders what she is dressing for. What could she do? What could be waiting for her? She's sweating; it's too hot already. Her cell phone rings on the floor and she picks it up.

"Hey, what's up?" Mallory sighs.

"I called in sick."

"Good for you. I got fired."

They agree to meet at Ray's in an hour, and Iris finishes getting ready. She swishes mouthwash while tying her shoes, humming through the stinging green liquid. She picks her big canvas tote bag from the top shelf of her closet and switches her belongings from her purse. She's sitting on the closet floor with her makeup and billfold, her keys and gum wrappers in piles around her, thinking how long it's been since she's organized anything, her bedroom a jumble of hastily stashed clothes, cheap, falling-apart shoes, and dust bunnies illuminated by sunbeams, when a loud rush of hissing snow comes blaring through the open door. She jumps up and rushes back to the living room, where the little radio leans against the arm of the couch, pervading the room with white noise. She snatches it up and jabs the off switch hard. Off— it's off this time— was it off before? The room is silent again, and Iris carries the radio back to her bedroom. She sets it on the dresser next to her stereo. She turns her stereo on, and Elvis is singing about suspicious minds. She looks at the radio beside her stereo, side by side, the one only two years old, black and a little imposing, her daily companion, the other one a flat gray, toy-like, and seemingly quite old, with a slightly bent antenna. She picks up the little radio, flips open the back and removes the batteries, tucking them away together in her top drawer as the horns swell brightly, trumpeting the day outside her smudgy window. She listens to the rest of the song standing against the dresser, her head resting on her folded arms.

She arrives at Ray's Coffee Shop before Mallory and finds a table upstairs, looking out over the bottom level. This way, she can see her when she comes in, and she can watch people unnoticed. She can stare right down at their heads in this wooden room, the walls, floor, ceiling, and tables all the same shade of wood, like the place was carved out of a single tree, then filled with soft red couches and stacks of newspaper. Most of the customers are alone, spines curved toward computer screens, books, or newspapers. She remembers that she has not read a real honest-to-god book in possibly months.

Mallory walks in to a clang of little bells and Iris waves down to her. She watches the top of her head as she orders her coffee.

A minute later, Mallory comes over and slumps into the chair opposite Iris. Her hair is in loose pigtails, a little greasy at the scalp, and she is wearing a heavy gray sweatshirt, though it is well over eighty degrees outside. She sets her cup down on the table, closer to Iris than to herself. She makes no move to drink from it.

"Here," Mallory says. "I don't want it."

"Oh, thanks," Iris says, gently pushing the cup to the side. "So."

"Yeah, so."

"Do you want to tell me what happened?" Iris asks.

Mallory rolls her eyes. "I just had to get out of the house. Sneering into the mirror isn't doing anything for me and Nathan is sick of looking at me like this."

"Nathan?"

"Nathan? My boyfriend? God, can you retain anything?"

"Oh. Sorry."

"Whatever. At least I'll get unemployment for a while. So freeing, right? I feel so unencumbered I could puke."

"I don't know. Sometimes I think about what I would do with my time if I didn't have a job. Haven't you? You could take a class, or learn how to do something..."

"I don't need to learn shit. I need to be able to pay my internet bill so I can keep judging celebrities' outfits."

"Yeah, of course."

The two sit in silence for a moment. The music over the speakers stops suddenly and Iris only then notices that there was music to begin with. Everyone in the café appears jarred out of something, eyes searching the silent air. A moment later the music is back, on a different radio station now, but filling the same need. A collective sigh of relief, masked now, unshared.

Mallory starts laughing, a loud, rollicking laugh. She doesn't seem to have noticed the shift.

"And the funniest part is," Mallory says, her laughter cooling, "I was going to quit anyway."

"What?"

"I'd been drafting my resignation letter in my head for months."

"Why?"

"Because I couldn't spend my life like that anymore, always under the gun, on deadline, we need this yesterday, like everything is life or death."

"I can't even imagine. So, then, it's a good thing you got fired?"

"No, because now I'm humiliated. And I didn't get to give her my awesome letter. I was going to call her Countess Bitchface."

"I don't know what I'd call my boss if I called him anything."

Iris thinks of the look on her boss's face as he examined the melons, holding them up to his ear as though attempting to crack a safe. She wonders where he is now, since he isn't where he said he'd be. He could be absolutely anywhere. She slumps down a little into her seat in case he's here.

"And now what?" Mallory continues. "It was always my plan to have some killer thing to leave for, to gloat about, and I waited too long." Slowly, her hard fuck-all expression gives way to a blank stare.

"Well," Iris says.

Mallory is looking at her fingernails.

"What would you do?" Mallory sighs, reaching for the coffee now, taking a long slug.

"What?"

"You said you've thought about what you'd do with all the extra time if you didn't have to work. So? What have you come up with?"

"Oh... nothing, I guess. I don't know what I was getting at. I was just trying to help."

"Then why'd you call in sick? You don't do that. Remember when you broke your wrist sophomore year? You went to Spanish before you went to the health center. I could hear you whimpering under your breath the whole time."

"I didn't break it. It was just a sprain."

Mallory leans back into her chair, regards her. "But you're not even sick, are you?"

"No, I don't feel good, really." If necessary, Iris believes she can will a cold to strike. A flu, if she concentrates hard enough. She could still do it.

"You look fine to me."

"It's my... throat. My throat hurts."

"Do you want some tea? I'll get it." Mallory starts to get up.

"No, don't. I'm fine."

"So you are playing hooky. Whole day. Free as a bird. What are you going to do with the time?"

"I don't know."

"You could call Marcus back. He said you never returned any of his calls." Mallory squints.

"I don't think he ever did call…" Iris thinks back and realizes she doesn't know if he's called or not, though she can't imagine why he would. She can't say she's been checking her phone very regularly, or always remembering to charge it. She's barely been paying attention to anything.

"Is there someone else you haven't told me about? Is that why you never call the guys I set you up with?"

"Hm?" Iris inhales sharply, "what?"

"You really don't pay a lot of attention," Mallory says, and Iris is startled, as though her thoughts have been broadcast aloud without her knowledge or consent.

"Do you?" she prods.

Iris remembers then, how to defuse things when Mallory starts to needle like this. How to distract her. She tries to mirror Mallory's smirk.

"You must be planning some sort of revenge, right? Against Countess… what was it?"

"Bitchface." Mallory's face softens a little into a smile, though her eyes remain narrowed. "I *would* like to let the air out of her tires."

"With what, like a switchblade?"

"With my goddamn incisors."

Iris laughs first, and Mallory follows, her teeth flashing.

"You could put sugar in her gas tank."

"Too pedestrian," Mallory sniffs.

"Superglue a quarter to her windshield, right in her field of vision? She wouldn't be able to get it off without cracking the glass."

"That's better."

"Or, you could wait until she goes out, sneak into her office, take her chair apart, and fill the legs with strips of raw meat. She wouldn't notice at first, probably. Not until the smell got really bad."

"She'd call building management and have them tear the whole place apart. You're sick."

"I told you I was." Iris clutches her throat and makes a wounded face, making the two of them laugh again.

Iris decides then what she's going to do today. She stops laughing as her own plans for a more benign sort of mischief begin to materialize.

"There's only one problem," Mallory says, grimacing.

"What's that?" Iris asks, staring vaguely at the wall behind Mallory.

"No. I could never get back into that building. I was escorted out by security."

"Why?"

"I said some stuff. I'm not telling you. You'll think less of me." Mallory narrows her eyes, pleased with herself as she takes another sip. "So. Now what?"

"I've got to go." Iris stands up from the table and heads for the stairs.

"You should print that on a business card," Mallory calls out.

Iris turns back with an apologetic smile, then continues down the stairs. She thinks it was a smile. She may have just swiveled her head, her face blank. But she can't worry about that now.

She steps out onto the street and the morning is settled now, sunny and stagnant. She walks around the corner to her car, shining in the too-close, too-hot sun.

In the car, Iris begins to lose nerve. The air conditioner is broken, so she rolls her windows down. The wind blows hard in her ears and sets her hair flying as she rolls through the wide boulevards. It drowns out the radio, so all she hears is the flap and roar.

She is not even sure what she is doing. She should keep driving. She should go back home, where she can't do any damage.

She should count her blessings that she has a job, a home, a car, working lungs, and a beating heart.

But she makes the turn into the parking lot, parking her car at the far edge, against a strip of concrete filled in with low hedges. But instead of crossing the lot to the building, she steps down the small driveway into the residential area that overlooks the main street below.

She walks past bright, clean houses, small dogs yipping in yards. She steps out into the street to avoid sprinklers that douse the sidewalk, missing their mark, while the lawns gape, parched. In her sneakers, she is able to negotiate the heaving lumps in the sidewalk, where roots push up and out, unstoppable.

She turns down toward the main thoroughfare, and finds herself walking alongside the vacant lot, the one that didn't used to be vacant. It is still empty. Emptier. The sign is gone.

I'm home. Are you?
I'm home. Where?
I'm home. So what?

She can see it sometimes, still, when she closes her eyes. She walks to the other side of the lot, her eyes never leaving the weedy ground inside the fence. There is no post. There is no hole in the ground. She grips the chain link in her fingers, searching for some sign of what she knows she saw, knows she did. The words exist only for her now. It is possible, probable, that no one else ever saw, because who else is looking off to the sides of things? Everyone she sees is facing forward, in motion toward a specific something. Her throat tightens and she swallows hard a few times, dry swallows, skin against skin.

She keeps walking, all the way to the hardware store several blocks west. She remembers it from a time her boss sent her to pick up a single 2-by-4, late on a Monday afternoon.

She wanders the aisles, sure of what she is looking for, but unsure of where it might be hidden. When she finds it, she approaches slowly, as though under surveillance. She can move so slowly that no motive can be assigned. She can move so slowly that any watcher would lose interest. This is where her power lies, and she is in just the right place now to claim it. She approaches the display, turns slowly on her heel to face it.

Iris doesn't know anything about drills. She flags down a sales associate.

"Excuse me," she says. "Can you tell me which drill bit will fit this one?" She holds the smallest power drill aloft, having chosen it for its smallish size, just the right fit for her purse.

"What kind of job is it?" he asks.

"The usual kind."

"Um…"

"Just whatever will fit."

"Okay," he shrugs, and pulls a package from the wall. She snatches it from his fingers, pays, and ducks into the alley behind the store to assemble the thing, her back up against the hot painted brick wall, parts splayed out in the gravel.

By the time she arrives back at the office building, she is sweaty, thirsty, and made of steel. She creeps around to the back of the building, where she scans the parking lot for her boss's car. She doesn't see it anywhere. But the white van is there, dirtier still, and parked under a small diseased-looking tree, its slack branches laid out on the windshield and hood.

Iris climbs the stairs softly, stopping when a woman she's never seen before passes her on the stairs carrying a stack of manila envelopes. She does not think it is beyond the realm of possibility that she is invisible when motionless. She has no evidence for or against. At the top of the stairs, she runs her hand over the jagged wall. It's true that it opens up the space. It does feel easier to breathe.

When she unlocks the door, she is met with the bray of the burglar alarm, reassurance that the suite is empty, though her arrival is now announced. As she slips inside, she glances back to make sure that the door of 2B is closed before punching in the code.

She walks through the suite, checking each empty yet cluttered room. These rooms should be locked, she thinks.

She returns to the front lobby area right in front of her desk. It has to be the storage room— the official one. The back wall of that room. That is the shared wall, the wall against which her European colleague used to lean his chair. Who was on the other side then? What switch was made? To make sure she has the space right in her head, she steps out into the hall, faces her door. She visualizes the wall as it extends beyond the door and back into the room, both rooms, 2A and 2B. As she re-enters the suite, she traces the wall with her hand until she is inside the storage room. She finds the spot.

Crouching between the boxes and the smooth white wall, Iris takes the tool out of her bag. She visualizes her mark, then takes out her Sharpie to draw a wet black X. She flips the switch and watches the drill whir and spin before touching it to the center of the X. Once she has made a hole, made contact with the air on the other side, she runs the drill along its edges to enlarge the hole, make it swell beyond its borders, create new borders with each pivot of her wrist.

When she is finished, she switches the tool off, blows on the wall, and leans forward on her knees. She puts her eye to the hole and blinks. What does she see?

It is hard to make out. She sees the green chair. She sees the lavender carpet, the same carpet she is kneeling on. But her field of vision is limited. A hole any bigger would attract notice. Still, she can tell that the room is empty, even if she can't see the whole room. There is a stillness. She unfocuses her eyes, and the air passing between the two rooms feels hazy and thin.

"There you are!"

The voice comes at her from behind and she jumps up onto her feet, letting the drill drop to the ground.

"Listen, I need this typed up within the hour— I'm already late." Her boss, in only his shirt and tie, no jacket, extends his arm toward her, waiting. She takes the notebook pages from his hand.

"Thanks," he calls back over his shoulder as he marches toward his office. "And make twelve copies!" She is still standing in the storage room.

She looks down at the pages in her hand. She leaves her things in the room and carries the pages to her desk. She sits down, and the leather sticks to her bare thighs. The air conditioning is turned up too high and she has no sweater. Every hair on her body stands on end. She turns on her computer, and it lights up with a soft chime. She lays the pages before her on the desk while the computer warms up. His handwriting is getting worse. She turns her head toward the hallway and wonders which door he came from. These pages are going to be difficult to interpret.

She begins typing. Once she is finished, and he has left for whatever he is already late for, she will reward herself by kneeling underneath the water cooler and sucking down water as fast as it will come. Until then, she is stuck to her chair.

Later, as her boss is walking out the door, he stops in front of her desk, where she sits brushing the keyboard with her two index fingers, the job done.

"You were late today," he says.

Iris squints up at him.

"About that," she begins, hoping he will reveal the tone of his comment before she has to finish the sentence.

"It won't happen again," he says, stepping on her line.

"No. No, it won't." She nods gravely, wondering if in fact he listens to any of his voicemail, ever.

"No. No it won't." He repeats, looking right into her eyes, and now she is not sure what they are talking about.

He maintains eye contact for a long moment before turning and opening the door out into the hall. When the door clicks shut behind him, she takes several long, full breaths. She gets up and hurries to the window that looks out over the parking lot and watches him get into his car, in his parking spot, his car which was not there before. She looked. She's sure of it. As sure as a person can be, which is almost sure. In any case, he is gone now.

Iris drinks several cupfuls of water before returning to the matter at hand. She enters the storage room, settles in front of the shared wall, and lines her left eye up with the small hole, her palms pressed to the wall on either side as though holding it still. Perhaps, she thinks, she could lift it up like a garage door or push it aside like a curtain. She wants a way into his space, like he's gotten into hers, without even seeming to try. Iris massages the wall with her palms, fostering its potential energy.

She blinks into the other room, her eyelashes brushing the upper edge of the hole. Her breath hits the wall and comes back at her, then back again, in an endless loop of humidity, a private tropical climate, one inch by one inch. Still, the other room remains empty, or, full of things that sit and settle as she is doing right now. Then there is the sound of a door opening, and thinking it is her boss returning, she pushes herself awkwardly up onto her feet and begins pretending to look for some office supply that she needs in order to do something or other, but no one comes, and she realizes it is 2B that someone has entered. She can hardly tell the difference between *here* and *there*.

Slowly, she lowers herself down again onto her knees and looks into the hole to see the man's gray trousers and black dress shoes. He is standing still, and Iris wonders if he is thinking, or just unsure what to do now. She wishes she could see all of him. There might have been a better way of doing this. If she had any technical savvy, she could have installed a hidden camera. But this is her way, and it will have to do.

She keeps watching, as he disappears, and returns with a large cardboard box, into which he places several folders. He disappears again, and returns with a newspaper-wrapped bundle in the shape of a lamp, which he then places gingerly into the box before taping it shut. Then he walks off again, taking the box with him, and doesn't come back.

Eventually, Iris pulls her face away from the wall, and for a moment, she forgets what she is waiting for— it's just her, alone in a room. But, remembering herself, she stands up, runs out of the room to the hall window and looks down onto the parking lot.

She watches as he places the box in the white van, then pulls out a stack of flat boxes, which he hitches under his arm and carries back to the building. Iris rushes back to the storage room and takes her place at the wall.

When she hears the door, and sees his bottom half re-enter the frame, she watches breathlessly, an invisible barricade at her windpipe forged out of sheer concentration. She watches, and listens to the rustle of old paper, as the map comes down from the wall. He rolls it up with his fists at waist-level, seeming to amble casually through the space and out of view. When he comes back, the map is gone. He has a tape gun in hand, and begins putting together another box.

Iris lets out a strange squeak of a gasp, then ducks away from the wall.

The man stops.

"Hello?" he says.

She burrows her face up against the carpet, her eyes squeezed shut.

"Hello?" he says again.

Iris lifts up her face and slowly brings it up to the hole again. He is closer now, and seems to be advancing, slowly, but with intent, in her direction. When he stops, she looks down at his shoes, just inches from the wall. If one could look at both rooms with just a cross-section of the flimsy drywall between them, there she would be, knelt at the man's feet, with him none the wiser.

"Hello?" he mutters softly this time, and Iris is close enough to hear it.

"Are you leaving now?" she answers, then covers her mouth.

"Who said that?"

"...me."

"Where are—"

Iris doesn't have to answer, because he quickly figures it out himself. He lowers himself to the floor, and his eyes lock onto her one.

"What did you say?"

"I asked if you were... leaving."

"I'm trying something," he says, after a moment.

"What?"

"I'm just trying something. You'll see."

"Have... have you really been living here?"

He sits up then, so her view stops at the bend of his waist, the tuck of his white shirt.

"You don't have to worry about it."

"I know I don't have to."

"I've got it under control."

She watches his breath move the thin fabric of his shirt.

"This is my wall, you know," he says.

"Only that side is," she says. "This side is mine."

He laughs then, a quiet, raspy laugh.

"True enou—"

"—Where are you going?" she interrupts.

"Nowhere. Not just yet."

"Oh."

For all the times she's longed to talk to him like this, her mind is racing, clawing for anything to say.

"Where did you come from?" she asks, finally.

There's a pause between the rooms.

"What are you after?" he asks.

"I..." she begins. She can't remember when she noticed the office next door was empty. She only noticed when it filled again, an anchor materialized, as though formed out of the air, for her to grab onto. But there was someone there before him, before her even, and another before that. When did she start needing an anchor? Walls lined with closed doors have trained her after all this time to perceive the weight of things she can't see. She closes her eyes and feels his weight on the carpet fibers on the other side of the wall.

"What are you after?" she counters.

His face is right there, though he doesn't look at her— she sees only the corner of his mouth and his rough chin.

"I can't explain it to you."

"Try."

"I've been trying to figure it out for a long time."

"If you tell me who you are, and what you've come here for," Iris begins carefully, "I'll listen."

"I know," he whispers, and Iris watches his mouth.

"Can I come over there?" she whispers back.

And before he can answer, the phone rings, and it triggers a reflex in her, snapping her out of the smallness they've created.

"Hold on," she says, "hold on—" her heart beating fast.

She jerks her head back from the wall. She takes a deep breath and scrambles to her feet to get to the phone.

"Larmax, Inc., how can I help you?"

"Um, hi. I don't know if this is the right number," a woman says.

"Um," Iris echoes, "how can I help you?"

"I'm calling about the job? The opening for a receptionist?"

"I'm the receptionist."

"Oh. Huh. What number is this?"

"487-2359."

"Hold on."

Iris listens to the rustling of paper.

"Oh," the woman comes back on the line, "my mistake," and hangs up.

Iris hangs up in turn and goes back to her water, but it goes down the wrong way when she takes a sip and leaves her coughing, a knot unfurling in her chest. Another phone rings somewhere else on the second floor, then another somewhere closer, but hers stays silent. She sits, shoulders hunched, on the edge of her desk for a long moment; her throat is raw again.

She returns to the storage room and kneels down at the hole. "Hello? Are you there?"

There's no answer. She brings her eye down to the hole, but she doesn't need to look to know he's not in there anymore.

But still, she steps out into the hallway and knocks on the door. She waits. She rattles the doorknob, then rattles it harder. She rests her forehead on the door for a moment. She doesn't recognize herself suddenly. She's on the verge of tears, but powerless to explain them. Her mouth feels dry and clumsy, incapable of forming words.

Why was she unable to let the phone ring? *I'm not even technically here*, Iris marvels, as she gathers her things and locks up. She must be programmed like a machine at this point, she thinks, an answering machine, but answering no call of any consequence. She jogs down the stairs and across the lot, hoping to get out quick and forget what she's done, distance pulling out the threads of her memory like she knows it can. She'll keep the windows down so speed can fill her ears with wind.

She can't imagine what time it is as she breathes hard. She focuses on her car in the distance, in the trajectory of the sprinklers that have started up to drown the hedges. Water sprays across the hood, and from here, she thinks she can make out a folded piece of paper nestled against the windshield. She runs faster, wisps of her hair fluttering against her mouth, and when she reaches the car, she pulls the damp paper very carefully out from under the windshield wiper, and unfolds it slowly so it won't come apart in her hands. Her eyes dart up and down the page hungrily, and she's thrown by the sheer volume of text and colorful images, little boxes in a vertical row. The ink is smeared, and she can't seem to catch hold of any meaning to the words, and the pictures are too small to make out— until gradually each element slides into place, and she realizes it's a flyer, for a new Jamaican restaurant down the street. She looks behind her and sees that there's one on every car in the lot. Feeling vulnerable, feeling stupid, she heaves herself into the car and throws the damp piece of paper onto the floor. She backs out quickly, careening down the driveway while another part of her, a part she is embarrassed to acknowledge even in secret, looks out the back, palms pressed to the window.

When she gets home, she sits in her car for a moment and listens to the cough of the engine— her poor, weak car, her dank garage, her small, tunnel-like world. She squeezes her eyes shut, grabs the flesh of her left forearm and pinches hard for as long as she can stand the sharp, rising throb of it, until her whole arm begins to pulse, gangrenous and foggy. Finally, she lets go, opening her eyes, and watches as the blotchy white skin regains its color.

DIGGING OUT

When she is inside, it feels so warm and muggy, she opens all the windows, unsealing the apartment. The air outside sends the curtains floating inward lackadaisically. She sits on the sofa, a hand-me-down from her parents, threadbare now but soft and smelling of pencil shavings and fireplaces. She plunges her face into the cushion and takes a deep whiff.

She should be tired but she isn't. Not at all. Her eyes are wide open and dry as chalk. She pops up onto her feet again and grabs the phone out of her purse. She dials Mallory.

"Hey," Mallory answers.

"Hey, what are you doing?"

"I've been cooking all day. I never cook, that's just how fucking bored I am. I made eggplant parmesan, spaghetti, bruschetta— do you wanna come over? We're never gonna be able to eat all of this ourselves. You should come help us eat— I don't want to get fat too on top of everything."

"Um, okay. What time? Should I bring something?"

"I don't know, seven? You don't have to bring shit."

"I probably will anyway."

"Fine, bring booze. Wait, hold on a second."

Iris hears the clack of the phone being placed on a hard surface. She waits there.

"Sorry sorry," Mallory returns with a clatter. "Listen, make it seven-thirty, okay?

"Okay, see you."

"Yeah, mmhhmm," Mallory says, hanging up quickly.

Iris looks at the clock on the stove. 5:48. She changes into jeans, ballet flats, and a bronze tank top. She drags her bag into the closet and dumps everything on the floor to switch her belongings into a smaller purse. The power drill falls out with a metallic thunk, her billfold and makeup clacking out along with it onto the closet's peeling hardwood. She picks up the drill and pushes it underneath a pile of sweaters on the closet floor.

Once dressed, she walks down to the corner store to buy a bottle of wine. It is still light out, but it's a tentative lightness. Dry leaves float past her down the sidewalk in the lazy breeze. She walks through the automatic doors and an electronic chime sounds, alerting the elderly man behind the counter to her arrival. She glances over at him, but he doesn't look up from his paper. The wine selection is extensive, one side of the store filled with random grocery items and miniature bottles of detergent, all emblazoned with faded orange price tags, the other side hooch heaven, the selection ranging from dusty bottles of Old Grand-Dad to Dom Pérignon locked in a glass case perched up high behind the counter. She paces sideways across the wine aisle, craning her neck to peruse the top shelves. She doesn't know anything about wine, so this perusal is for show, though no one is watching but the blinking red security camera behind the counter. The real decision is between the three cheapest cabernets, on the bottom shelf, each one under nine dollars. She chooses the one with the most austere gold lettering on its label.

Iris steps outside onto the sidewalk carrying the bottle by its neck in a paper bag and turns the corner back onto her street. The moment she turns, she is met by a giant Great Dane, leonine almost in its grace, its gray fur glowing in the not-yet moonlight. Sitting up straight on the sidewalk before her, its head practically reaches her chest. She stops and looks into its droopy brown eyes.

"Hi," she says.

The dog stares back at her. Slowly, she reaches out a hand.

"Here," she whispers, "here." The dog looks at her hand but makes no move to sniff it. She inches closer and slowly moves her hand from in front of the dog's face to the top of its head.

"Okay?" she asks, lightly touching the soft fur on the top of the dog's head with her fingertips. She feels the outline of its skull. The dog doesn't react, but allows her to continue petting. She rubs her whole hand on its head, then smoothes its ears back. At this, the dog closes its eyes in pleasure.

"Who are you?" she asks. The dog has a tag, and she leans down to read it.

"You have a very sophisticated name, Federico." She looks back into the dog's eyes. His ears have perked up at the uttering of his name.

Still petting his head, Iris looks around for a possible owner, someone running, frantic, dragging an empty leash, slack against the pavement. There is no one, anywhere.

"I guess you'd better come with me," she says, "and we can call that phone number on your tag."

She pauses then, wondering how exactly she will coax Federico into following her. There is no way that she could pull him, so he needs to follow of his own volition. She takes a few steps toward home and looks back. The dog has turned his head to watch her, but he hasn't stood up.

"Are you coming?" she asks. "Are you coming, Federico?" He tilts his head to the left.

She takes another few steps and stops. When she turns, Federico is standing, still facing her. She locks her eyes onto his.

"Yeah," she says, "like that. Keep going like that."

She takes another few steps, and when she turns, Federico is just a few feet behind her, following with a worried look on his face, brows pinched and watery brown eyes wide.

He follows her all the way to her apartment building, and

waits patiently while she unlocks the front door. She steps in, but he stays outside the threshold.

"Come on," she says, "you have to follow me. You have to follow me all the way in." He stays where he is, staring past her, she thinks, down the long hallway that stretches past the mailboxes.

"Federico," she says, and at this he follows. She lets the door swing shut behind them and leads him up the stairs to her apartment. He moves up alongside her as they climb the stairs. She scratches his neck and imagines that they are long-estranged friends reunited, slightly dazed in the revisiting of old habits.

By the time they get inside the apartment, Federico seems comfortable and quickly begins sniffing the floor, walls, and furniture, barely containing his excitement. He disappears down the brief hallway to her bedroom, tail wagging.

"I know," she says, "I know."

Satisfied with his inspection, the dog rushes back to her, panting. He is so comically huge, he makes her already small apartment look doll sized. She rubs his cheeks with both hands and he melts, his eyes closing as he lowers himself to the carpet. Iris follows, curling up against him.

"I know," she says, "I know," and his fur is so soft. She lays her head on his back and hears the bellow of his colossal heartbeat. He outweighs her by at least thirty pounds and smells like dirt, as though he sprouted and grew in a garden she never knew was there, just waiting to be found.

She closes her eyes and breathes him in, falling asleep amid visions of black soil and cool, wet grass, the great magnet at the earth's center locking it all in place. As she falls further into sleep, the magnet tightens. Instead of locking the earth in place, it is sucking everything back to its center with a grinding force that builds. Lying prone, she can feel her ribs as they loosen and pull apart from her skeleton. The ground begins to shake, and she feels her veins untangle as every part of her prepares to go under.

Iris wakes with a start to find herself splayed out face down on the carpet, Federico stretched out over her legs, pinning her. Her legs are numb below the knee. She panics.

"Federico! Get off!"

The dog casually stands up and Iris flips over onto her back and lurches her top half up like a spring as the blood returns to her legs in sharply tingling waves. She hugs her legs to her body and moans, "Owowowowow."

"We'd better call your family, Federico," she moans. "They must be worried sick." The dog cowers as though he has done something wrong. Iris punches her calves and squints against the cave-like darkness of her living room.

When her legs have recovered, she stands up, switches on the light and heads for the kitchen phone. She calls the dog to her and consults his tag while she dials. While it is ringing, she glances at the clock on the stove and is shocked to see that it is 8:15 already. The phone continues to ring, and she is frazzled, disoriented, still. Federico lays his head on her left foot with the weight of a bowling ball. The call goes to voicemail and Iris hangs up.

"Oh no," she says aloud, and Federico lifts his head up at her. She looks back at him, his black nose twitching.

"I bet you're hungry," she sighs.

She fills a bowl with cereal, no milk, and another with water.

"Here," she says, placing the bowls on the floor, "that's almost like kibble, right?"

While he drinks the water with gusto, splashing it all over the kitchen floor, she picks up the phone and hits redial. This time, a woman answers after three rings.

"Hello?"

"Hello? Are you missing a Federico?"

"You found him?! Where are you? I'll be right there— is he

okay?" the woman on the other end can barely get one sentence out before she interrupts herself. She sounds like she is halfway out the door already, lumbering toward a car.

"I'm at 1404 Kenmore— Kenmore and Lexington?"

"You're kidding."

"No? No, I'm not kidding."

"That's a good six miles from here. I didn't even put up flyers that far out."

"Oh, well he's okay. He's fine."

"Hang on— I'll be right there."

Iris hangs up and looks at Federico sitting in front of her, wagging his tail across the kitchen floor, both bowls depleted behind him in a torrent of gnashes and licks. She thinks he looks proud.

"Oh god," she yawns. She steps into the bathroom and turns on the light. Her face is a mess of red indents from the carpet. She stares into the mirror and gives her cheeks a few light slaps while opening and shutting her eyes to wake up. The dog licks her elbow and she lets him do it. She brushes her hair and feels lopsided, one arm dry, the other coated in Federico's sticky slobber and the musky fog of his breath.

About thirty minutes later, the kitchen phone rings and it is Federico's owner downstairs. Iris buzzes her in.

She opens the door to a tall older woman with ruddy skin and frizzy gray hair pulled into a long ponytail. Despite the warm weather, she wears a yellow raincoat. She must be outdoorsy, Iris thinks. Federico runs to the door and the woman sinks to her knees and embraces him while he buries his snout between her neck and shoulder.

"Rico! Rico, it's you!"

"How long has he been missing?" Iris asks.

The woman looks up at her, arms still wrapped around the dog. "It's been over three weeks."

"Jesus."

"He seems to have done well for himself," the woman says, feeling his sides. She pulls a leash and harness out of the zippered pocket of her raincoat and pushes it gently over the dog's head. He instinctively steps through the leg openings. "Lord knows how," she sighs, rising to her feet. Her smile looks as though it might crack her skin.

"Listen," the woman says, still in the hallway, Federico now at her side. Iris wonders if she should invite her in, but it seems too late for that. "I can't thank you enough for calling. We figured we'd probably never see him again."

It hits Iris then that she will never see him again. Nor will she ever see this woman again. How many others fall into this category, she wonders. How many faces of strangers are stored in her memory— how many faces she'll never have the opportunity to recall? There is so much slippage, so many faces, voices, thoughts stored within but inaccessible, lost in the folds. She wants to tell the woman that she almost didn't call. That maybe she would have kept him with her always. He would sit under her desk at work, his tail jutting out to trip her boss. She would lay out laundry on his back, feed him hamburgers. But it wouldn't be true. None of that ever occurred to her. She watches the woman's hands worrying the leash.

"Well, thanks again, really. God bless." She turns down the hall, Federico trotting beside her.

"Wait!" Iris shouts, too loud.

The woman and the dog both turn.

"How did he get out?"

"Oh. He dug his way out. I found the tunnel going right under the fence when I got home."

"Okay," Iris nods, not sure why she asked. She watches the dog's face. *Come back*, she thinks. *You can stay forever if you just come back.* He stares back at her, mouth wide, then buries his face into his owner's jacket.

"Don't know why he bothered," the woman continues. "He

could've jumped clean over it if he'd wanted to, tall as he is. Some kind of instinct, I guess."

"I was just curious," she says, still looking at him and not her.

"Well, goodnight," she says, "we'd better go home. Right, Rico?"

"Yeah, goodnight," Iris says, leaning against the door. As she closes it behind her, she hears the woman murmuring softly to the dog, but she can't make out the words.

She attempts to clean up her face with tissue and more makeup. The apartment feels exceedingly quiet, every sound muffled by carpet and insulated walls. Nothing she does makes any sound. She stamps her foot on the bathroom floor to interrupt the quiet, but it is a pitiful scuff against the vast silence within these walls. "Fuck," she says, restless. The clock on her cell phone reads 8:50 and Mallory lives a good twenty minutes away. As late as she is, she can't seem to hurry. She tries, but the simple mechanics of movement seem to require so many steps. Everything requires a separate motion, bending to adjust a shoe, picking up a purse, running fingers down strands of hair, catching them in tangles. She is maddeningly aware of all of it. And then, she stops. She drops her purse on the bathroom floor, leaves her reflection hanging in the mirror, and goes back out to the living room, where she tries to call Mallory, but no one picks up.

She opens the wine and pours herself a tall mug, standing at the counter. She is trying to clean up the mess of Federico's bowls with her toes, collecting the stray bits of cereal when the expected call from Mallory comes, and Iris leans on the counter and picks up, bracing herself.

"Uh, hi," Mallory says, "what time is it where you are?"

"I'm really sorry. There was this dog, and…"

"Right," she interrupts curtly, startling Iris.

"I know. I really am sorry…"

"Well come now then."

"I just, I can't do it. I'm sorry."

"Jesus H.," Mallory whispers, "this poor guy drives all the way over here—"

"What guy?"

"Ugh, he's a co-worker of Nathan's— Alan, very cute, tall…"

"Mallory, I'm not a good project for you. You ought to know that by now." Iris sips her cheap wine and feels its granules clinging to her top row of teeth.

"Oh, for crying out loud. It's dinner. It's drinks. It's conversation, nothing easier in the world."

"I know. I know that. But, just stop trying so hard."

"I'll stop trying once you start trying at all," Mallory almost hisses now, quietly. Iris hears the whoosh of a sliding glass door. "I'm sick to death of explaining you to people."

"So don't."

"Maybe I shouldn't."

Neither says anything for a few moments and Iris wonders if this is a fight, and what she's supposed to say now.

"I said I was sorry," she tries.

"Yeah. Look, I don't care what you do, it's just— we're going to be old someday and I'm afraid you'll wind up some lonely old bat."

"Because it would reflect poorly on you?"

She hears the click of Mallory's cigarette lighter.

"No. Maybe."

"Why don't you give up, then?"

"Maybe I should have asked myself that very question a long time ago."

"I've got to go."

"Oh, chill out, forget I said anything. Just come have one drink? Just one?"

"I can't. I'll… I'll talk to you later or something." Iris hangs up, afraid of what she might say to push Mallory over the edge into writing her off completely.

She pulls the phone away from her ear, and Mallory says, "Oh for fuck's—" before Iris hits the button, cutting her off.

She drinks alone, standing on her balcony. More new graffiti has sprung up on the opposite wall: a jagged row of pointy stars of varying sizes that stretches along the whole side of the building, like a child's drawing of the night sky. She looks up to compare, but the stars above are few and patternless.

A second mug of wine makes her drowsy, and she all but sleepwalks to her bed, managing only to remove her shoes and jeans before crawling under the covers, and she's out.

For several hours, Iris is a slab of meat on the bed, her consciousness totally absent. Iris has left the building. She might as well be dead if not for the invisible fog of her breath and the small spot of drool on her pillow. But in the earliest morning, when the sun is daring itself to come up again, the lights inside of her fade back in.

* * *

It is cold in the dusty alley beside the house where Iris stands watch. It is late at night, but there are no stars in the sky.

Way out in the middle of the yard, her father is standing in front of the fig tree, staring up at the wide expanse of its spidery branches, its leaves in crackling piles at his feet. An axe dangles from his right hand.

Iris steps up a little closer, quietly, so he won't hear her. When she gets to the back porch, she sees her mother's face in the kitchen window. She's watching too.

Slowly, her father raises the axe and drives in hard into the trunk, but the sound it makes is a metallic clank, harsh, and echoing like a tuning fork.

Iris looks to her mother, who still watches intently. She's inside. She didn't hear just how loud it was. Sebastian comes around the side of the house and sits at attention by Iris's feet. She reaches down and rubs behind his ears.

Her father rears back with the axe a second time, swings with all his strength and this time, the sound of struck metal sounds, then reverberates, louder and louder out into the night. Iris covers her ears, and Sebastian rises to his feet and begins bucking his head forward and back, then he stops and lets out a clipped howl.

Her father drops the axe and steps slowly backward, as the tree vibrates before him as though electrified.

Iris creeps away, back against the side of the house. The tree is still ringing its warped, tinny ring, the only sound in the whole sleeping neighborhood. She approaches the street, running her fingers along the side of the house. Her fingertips are covered in soot as she looks out and sees neighbors' lights turning on, and some windows opening. She presses her back to the side of the house in an effort to merge with it, to limit her exposure. She turns her face away from the light of the neighbors' windows, more switching on, one by one— she can feel their glow on her neck, and on the backs of her bare arms.

With the sound growing, lowering so Iris can feel it weakening her knees, and the lights flicking, flicking, she feels utterly stuck. There will be no moving from this spot, not now, not ever, and then she thinks, *where is my brother?*

This sudden thought moves her to look back toward the street, but then the street is gone. In a second it's all gone. Even she is gone, a slab of meat on the bed once more, with the dawn rising outside.

REVOLUTIONARY

The CEO of Creationeers Tech looks like a turtle. He's saying something, but Neil has a hard time listening, distracted
by his little chin and beaky mouth.

"Mr. Finch?"

"Yes?"

"You can tell me a little bit about it now, if you're ready."

"Of course, absolutely," Neil says. *Yeah, just say whatever affir-
mative words come to your lips, asshole, yes, most assuredly*, he thinks,
blinking fast. He closes his eyes briefly to settle them down.

Neil pulls out his briefcase and plops it down onto the shiny
oak desk with a thump that makes the CEO, Mr. Krebs, jump
in his seat a little.

"What we have here," he says, "is a product meant to revolutionize the effects of sleep." He pulls out the puffy blindfold
and holds it out across the table, displaying it as though his palm
were a silver tray. Mr. Krebs takes it and turns it over in his
hands, his face expressionless.

"Do you want to try it first, or do you want me to tell you
more about it?"

Mr. Krebs looks up and nods, "Please, go on, go on."

"All right. Well— the product doesn't have a name yet, that'll
be up to you, but essentially, what it does is block out light while
providing a soothing white noise effect for the user. It's meant to
create an ideal sleep space, to put the user in… into that space."

Mr. Krebs sets the product down. "And this is going to, you said, revolutionize sleep? How do you mean?"

"Well," Neil begins, thinking, *I mean it's hyperbole, like we all shovel back and forth to each other all goddamn day like anything actually does anything,* "what I mean by that is that… the purpose of sleep is to renew the user. What we're trying to emphasize is the fact that perfect sleep is the way to personal betterment."

"Mmm, yes. And what do you mean, 'perfect' sleep? What does this," he holds up the puffy blindfold, "have to do with that?"

This used to be easy, the pitch. Something is blocking his flow, like a plug in the dam. He visualizes water flowing and takes a deep breath, which comes out too loud when he releases it, like a grunt. He swallows.

"Would you like to try it out? Just slip it on and press the button by your right ear."

Mr. Krebs complies, and Neil watches his slack, unsmiling mouth and folded arms. *Fuck you too, moneybags.* These thoughts keep butting in.

"What do you think?" he finally says.

"Okay, I've got it," Mr. Krebs says, slipping the blindfold off and pushing it across the table.

"And, what did you think?"

"Listen, Mr. Finch. It's a perfectly solid product; I won't try to argue otherwise. But it's very much like a product we already carry, which is already very much like a lot of products on the market."

"I see," Neil says, looking intently at the CEO's pursed little mouth.

"I mean," the CEO continues, "if you could convey to me what makes this different, well, then we might have something."

"What makes it different. It's, well, it's meant to be transformational, sir. The sounds have been meticulously designed to… lull the user, in, in a— maybe you'd like to take the product home? Try it out for a night. I guarantee you'll see what makes this a must-have item. Tell me, do you have trouble sleeping?"

"I sleep fine."

"If you don't want to take it now, I could have it delivered to your home?"

"No, no that won't be necessary."

A long silence sits like a boulder on the table while Neil tries to situate himself in the room and the conversation. He can barely remember anything he's said. He looks around the room, the shiny brown table and matte brown walls everything brown, brown, brown, *like this guy's opinion holds any more weight than anybody else's, like this guy's some kind of taste-maker with his finger on the pulse of the all-important market.* All he can think of to say is what he's actually thinking, always a no-no.

"Why did you want to meet with me, Mr. Krebs?" he asks, too pointedly.

He shrugs defensively, "I thought it might be interesting, but it turns out it isn't."

"What would've been interesting?"

"Excuse me, Mr. Finch?"

"Is there something you're able to imagine that this product could've been, some imaginary product to whose image this actual product doesn't measure up?"

Mr. Krebs looks at Neil, hard, and cocks his head to one side as though something has just come to his attention.

"I think we're done here," he says.

Mr. Krebs then gives Neil an admonishing look that momentarily enrages him, but he collects himself, unsure suddenly what he's said versus what he's thought.

"Good, good," he says, standing. He shakes Mr. Krebs's hand across the table and shoves the blindfold into his briefcase. "Good to meet you, great," he says, without making any eye contact, and leaves the room.

Neil takes the stairs down to the building's garage, too

impatient to wait for the elevator. He forgot to get his parking pass validated, so he'll have to pay for it out of pocket, seven dollars for not a goddamn thing. His anger returns for a moment, as he climbs into his rented silver Nissan, making him heave himself into the car and slam the door hard, but it subsides as he sits behind the wheel for a moment, key poised at the ignition.

He realizes he doesn't care. Of course he doesn't care. When has he ever cared? He pretends to care so much that he almost fools himself into believing he really does. Almost.

He stows the key in the ignition but doesn't turn it, instead pulling the blindfold out of his briefcase. He slips it onto his face, leans back, and presses the button. After a couple of seconds, a soft rattle starts up, followed by a low whoosh, then slowly another little rattle. He's disoriented at first, trying to put an image to the noise, until it becomes clear to him that he's listening to a rain stick tipping back and forth. He pictures the stick turning slowly against a hazy black backdrop. He spaces out to the image, but before long, he's picturing the stick in someone's hand, some intern in a gray studio, holding the stick up to a grungy microphone, and he starts laughing.

He keeps laughing, blindfolded in his car, in the vast, echoing garage, under the hulking twenty-story office building.

Revolutionary, he thinks, *a revolution in personal regeneration and success.* This makes him laugh even harder, until tears are rolling out from under the velvety fabric of the blindfold.

The Pattern

Iris climbs into her car in the dark garage and turns the ignition. It sputters as though out of habit or not up to the task after being abandoned for a weekend she spent holed up, hermit-like. She tries again and it starts with a coughing rumble.

She parks at the office, happily a whole fifteen minutes early, the traffic having been oddly light. She uses the time to grab a latte and a blueberry muffin down the street. Walking back to the office, the coffee cup warm in her hand and white paper bag clutched in her fingers, she is glad to be out. In these moments, out in the world, when it is obvious to anyone who she is— a worker, a working girl, a commuter, a morning person blending in seamlessly in line at the café— she relaxes. Everything has been decided, in these moments. It is easy to be in these places. It is so easy to walk the streets in the bright, cool morning sun, with rush hour traffic whizzing by and a destination straight ahead.

As she fiddles with the lock of the office door, she can't help glancing at 2B. She noticed that the white van was in the same spot in the parking lot, collecting more and more debris from various flora, carried by the thick breeze. He hasn't gone anywhere, not yet. She gets the door unlocked and the alarm shrieks until she punches in the code by touch, out of habit, her gaze still floating toward the other door. *Unless he's abandoned the car*, she thinks. It could stay there forever, sink roots into the pavement, its owner long gone, and she would be the only one to notice.

Finally, she disengages from the door and puts her muffin and coffee down on her desk. She sets the office alight, the long fluorescent tubes activating behind grates across the ceiling, one to the next like dominoes falling, until the last one at the far end of the hall doesn't light up, but flickers briefly and dies.

She sits behind her desk and pulls the muffin out of its crinkling paper while her computer turns on. Once again, there are no phone messages, but she is not too perturbed. It is just one less thing for her to bother with. No email either. A long line of one less things. She takes a slow sip of her coffee and rests her eyes on the desk in front of her. She reaches out her pinkie finger and tries to wipe dust from the grooves of her telephone key pad with the edge of her nail, but she can't get in there. There are things that can't be cleaned, things that stick around, untouchable and untouched. She eats her breakfast slowly, wholly contained in the bubble surrounding her neat and orderly desk, a shield of wood and snaking gray wires between herself and anything beyond.

She is still eating when her boss walks in, quickly shuts the door, and pauses. His back against the door, he looks to her with pleading eyes, she thinks at first, quavering and wide, his cell phone clutched to his chest. A purple vein appears on his forehead, bisecting his sweaty complexion. Gobsmacked, she holds his gaze, struggling to keep her own expression neutral yet open, ready to produce whatever reaction he expects from her. He looks on the verge of asking a question, but makes no sound. Finally, his uncertain mouth settles into a hard line and his eyes narrow.

"Don't eat in here," he says, shaking himself away from the door and hustling down the hall.

Iris finishes her last bite and shoves the paper bag into the wastebasket as her boss slams his door.

He has slammed his door on many occasions. He slams his door when the mail is late, even as he leaves stacks of it unopened on his desk. He slams his door when it starts raining, as though the weather is a personal affront. He slams his door, she thinks, just for the sound of it. It isn't for her benefit. But she has never seen his face like that, his eyelids fluttering, looking to her, she thinks, for help more vital than he can express, before slamming his face shut, just like the door.

She sits, staring down the hallway until he re-emerges from his office and comes marching toward her desk.

"Listen," he says, running both hands through his hair until it looks blown back by a rough wind. A rough wind made of grease.

"Yes?"

"We're going to close early today. I mean, I'm going to close early today. And you can too. So I'm going to go, now. Okay? Right." He punctuates this with a quick nod, then shuffles in his spot as though no direction holds what he's looking for. No direction is the right one. Finally, he trundles down the hall back to his office.

Iris begins tentatively gathering her things, not yet ready to commit to the idea of leaving. She has an irrational suspicion that if she leaves, he will come looking for her at her desk, the preceding conversation wiped clean from his memory. It may not be wholly irrational.

Then she remembers that Friday was payday, and she never got her check. She just paid her utilities and credit card bill, and her account balance is down to approximately zero. She goes to her boss's open door and knocks, standing sheepishly at the threshold.

"What?" he yells, his voice sounding as though it is coming from deep inside some hole.

Iris steps further into the room, still holding herself a little at bay in the doorframe. Her boss is hidden behind his desk.

"I was just wondering if I could get my check before you go?"

He pops his head up above the desk. "Check," he repeats, as though the word is new in his mouth. "Right, right."

He stands up and brushes off his pant legs, runs his hands compulsively through his hair again. "Right," a definitive nod.

She waits while he rummages through his desk and finally pulls out a big leather binder, turns to a page near the end and writes out a fresh check in her name. Since she began working here, the checks have always been handwritten like this. Until this moment, she has never thought it odd, maybe because they usually just appear on her desk every other Friday in a crisp windowed envelope. Now she wonders why payroll isn't filtered through corporate. For a second, a rush of questions she might ask raise themselves, Iris's unfocused stabs at mental organization, like *where* is corporate and *what* is corporate and *where is it you're always going?* But once the check is in her hand, the questions dissipate like blown dust, and really, the answers don't matter much.

"Turn the lights off when you go."

Iris looks up from the check in her hand and follows him out to the lobby, his gray suit jacket, briefcase, and clutch of folders a jumble in his hands.

"Wait," he says, pausing in front of her desk. "Don't turn off the lights."

"Okay."

He looks into her eyes, lowering his chin, as though waiting for her to say something else to assure him that she has understood. She keeps nodding.

"I'll know if you turn them off. If I come back and find them off, then I'll know."

"Right. Of course." Iris folds up the check into a small rectangle and tucks it into the barely functional front pocket of her skirt.

"Good," he says, halfway out the door, "good," and he's gone. She rushes to the window and watches as he hurriedly climbs into his convertible and drives away. She pulls the check out of her pocket and smoothes it, returning to her desk to slip it into her wallet.

Alone in the office now, Iris opens the door to the darkened storage room. She kneels down to peer through the hole in the wall, and is met by a wash of whiteness. It takes her a moment to perceive the texture of fabric, and another to realize that she is looking at a shirt. She pulls her face back. His breath— if it is his breath— moves the fabric ever so slightly in and out, against his skin, against the wall, and there is nothing else to see. He is blocking whatever else might be happening. She brings her ear to the hole, hoping to hear his breath, but no luck. She brings her mouth to the hole and breathes, and wonders if he feels a draft.

"Hello?" she tries.

No answer comes.

She tries again, louder: "Hello?"

Nothing.

It occurs to her that if she were to push her finger through the hole, supposing her finger was long enough, she might find the shirt empty, hung as a decoy, the man having escaped to some hidden room, one she has not yet managed to penetrate. This thought stops her. There is no end to what she doesn't know. If she were to fashion a hook and catch hold of the shirt, yank it down, another could be hanging just behind it, out of her reach, a self-regenerating series of veils.

Then there is a rumble of motion on the other side of the wall, and her view is suddenly unblocked. She looks into the empty room, lavender carpet, white walls and nothing else. Sun filters in through the shadeless window. But there is no sign of him.

"Hello?"

After a long silence, from somewhere, a voice, his voice, quietly says, "Please…"

"Please what?"

"Please… don't."

"Don't what? I can barely hear you."

"Please, don't worry."

"What?"

And he doesn't answer. She stares through the hole for a while longer, but nothing else happens.

Iris gets up and pulls a blank sheet of paper from a package by the door and brings it back to her desk.

With her Sharpie, she writes on three lines:

Please don't go yet.

My name is Iris.

I want to talk to you.

Her hand shakes as she writes the third line, and then, hovering over the paper, the marker in her hand suspended a centimeter above the page, she quickly writes out her phone number, and then blows on it to dry the ink. When she runs her fingers over the words and they don't smudge, she rolls the paper into a tight baton and goes back to the storage room, dampening the note slightly with her sweating palm. She kneels down, and watching her hands closely, pushes the paper through the hole. She thinks she hears it land against the carpet, and waits for a moment for a possible retrieval, but none comes. She stays kneeled there for a little longer, listening for anything. Finally, her knees cramping, the skin pressed painfully against the floor, she leaves the room and closes the door behind her, squeezing the metal handle, hot in her fist.

I'd better go, she thinks, *I'd better get out of here.*

On her way out, lights, appliances, and computer on, she begins setting the burglar alarm, but stops and presses the green button to erase what she's punched in. If she is following a pattern, then it makes sense to leave the alarm off. What is supposed to be off is on, so what is supposed to be on should remain off. This balance needs to be maintained or the pattern falters, and without the pattern, there is nothing to follow. She steps out, almost leaving the door unlocked, but this last habit, she can't break. She stabs her key in the hole and gives it a grinding turn, then tries the doorknob a few times, unconvinced of her ability to do anything and have it be done.

ACCUMULATION

On the way home, she pulls into the bank to deposit her check. There's a sign on the ATM outside that says it's out of service, so she steps inside the bank for the first time in possibly years. The music floating down from the overhead speakers is subtle, a completely ignorable slip of violin, and the air is goosebump cold. Iris fills out a deposit slip, endorses the check, and tucks both into an envelope, which she slides into a deposit kiosk.

The floor, walls, and glass partitions of the bank are sparkling clean, like the whole thing was carved out of liquid. But on the way to the exit, Iris spies a ceiling fan overhead, turning very slowly, and heavy with dust. Each edge of the fan is lined with a thick layer of gray muck. The fan groans a little with each turn. Who knows how thick it is on top, out of sight. She thinks about how dirty the air must be to have this effect. They are all breathing in this dust every second of every day. She can feel it, the filth sticking to the walls of her lungs. Noting the suggestion box by the door, Iris grabs another deposit slip and writes on the back with her Sharpie:

Don't forget about what's in the air.

She drops it in the box and steps outside, the late breakfast and early lunch crowds beginning to fill the streets. She gets back into her car and is no longer one of them. She is sealed off from the day out there. She starts the car and Tommy James is singing *crimson and clover, over and over* with that sonic tremble effect, and in her head, the sun dims and brightens in time.

Good, Good

In a towel, with a toothbrush hanging out the side of his mouth, Neil stands at his dresser tossing rolled socks across the room into an open suitcase on the unmade bed. If there's anything more fun than packing, he doesn't know what it is. He throws in one more pair of socks and then steps into the bathroom, swishing the toothpaste water in his puffed cheeks for a few seconds before spitting into the sink. He clicks his tongue, his mouth fresh and icy.

Next he moves onto clothes, weighing different outfits in his head, the gray suit, the navy blue suit, the black pants without pleats, the ones with pleats, ties steel gray, maroon, and marigold. He lays them all in the suitcase so he has plenty of options, throwing in a lint roller in the outside pocket, nail clippers, razor, comb, trench coat because the weather is unpredictable everywhere you go, better bring an umbrella too, and can't forget underwear, boxers, briefs, and boxer briefs, because you never know what your body's going to feel like wearing when you wake up. He pauses to vigorously towel dry his hair and the phone rings. He grabs it off the dresser and answers without looking to see who it is.

"This is Finch."

"Finch, Mason. You got a sec?"

"Uh, just a sec. I'm packing."

"Right. Listen, I just wanted to talk to you about the meeting with Creationeers."

"Yeah?"

"Nothing to be too concerned about, I just thought you should know so you could keep it in mind for future reference."

"What is it?"

"Obviously you know we didn't close the account."

"Yeah…" Neil sits down on the bed.

"Well, I had a talk with Krebs to see if I could change his mind, and he… shared his impressions. Of you."

"Impressions."

"Listen, don't worry too much about it, but he said you made him feel uncomfortable."

"Uncomfortable. Huh."

"He said he couldn't put his finger on it— just something about your demeanor, your 'intensity,' he called it. Again, this is just something to keep in mind."

"So, you're asking me to just keep in mind the fact that I somehow, in some ineffable way, made someone uncomfortable."

"Hey, hey, it's no big deal— no need to get up in arms about—"

"Up in arms? Who's getting…? I'm fine. That's fine. Is that it?"

Mason doesn't say anything.

Neil steps into the bathroom, where he looks into the mirror, watching himself on the phone. He blinks fast, then slowly, listening to Mason's long silence.

"I'm just asking you to keep it in mind," he says, finally. "Maybe you just need to relax, do some deep breathing exercises, take up yoga or something."

"Or something." Neil squeezes the phone. "Well thanks, Mason. Thanks for telling me. Duly noted."

"Hey, I'm just here to help you succeed, right? You okay?"

"I'm great."

"Good, good. I'll check in with you later in the week, all right?"

"Talk to you soon."

Neil hangs up the phone and tosses it into his briefcase. He stands there for a moment, staring at the suitcase beside it. He gets dressed and grabs some more clothes out of the closet, and a few pairs of shoes he wraps up in dry cleaner bags. He zips open the extender so he can fit in a few more things, some books, magazines, his still-wet toothbrush and paste, deodorant, band-aids, more socks because you can never have too many, more underwear too, why not bring all of it, a few different pairs of sunglasses, and then in his briefcase, his laptop, notes, planner, his checkbook, a couple rolls of cash, a folder containing his Social Security card and passport, a few of the blindfold prototypes, a blank pad of hotel paper that's sitting on the bedside table, and then rattling around loose he tosses in eye drops, breath mints, gum, a watch he never wears, a few pens he finds around the apartment, some loose change, a button.

He stops packing for a second and realizes that he's sweating. He looks in his hand, a bunched up yellow tablecloth he was about to stuff into the outside pocket of his suitcase. He'd pulled it off the table, letting a stack of mail scatter onto the floor. He drops the tablecloth on the bedroom floor and gets down on his knees, rubbing his eyes. He wipes the sweat from the back of his neck with an angry swipe.

Where am I going, where am I going, where am I going... he thinks, rubbing his scalp, because in order to pack he needs to know where in the fuck it is that he's going. He lost track somewhere along the way. He closes his eyes and sees himself driving, driving cross-country, passing by so many towns that used to be, towns with train tracks that stop abruptly at the outskirts, the steel ends gnarled up like bony fingers, towns that have been vacated because the jobs dried up, filled with abandoned houses with doors warped shut and closed-up drug stores with merchandise useless on dusty shelves, and little graveyards, with no one left to tend them, the sludge of dead flowers in piles.

He stands up again, and begins removing items from his luggage. The extra suits, the magazines, pens and paper, coasters off the coffee table, he shovels things out onto the floor with a cupped hand.

My demeanor. My intensity. That's it. He's just too intense, whatever that means. Was it that intensity that made it so easy for people to believe he'd done something unspeakable all those years ago, something worlds more sinister than noticing too late that the branch was straining, that the fall would send the boy catapulting into the sharp maze of branches below, that his neck would snap with a sound like metal against metal, a ringing smack that would carry through the whole yard and beyond? And was it intensity that led him, instantly, unconsciously, to scrape his own hand hard against the tree, drawing blood, his idea of evidence that he'd tried to do something, and failed?

He's emptied the suitcase, its contents flung about the room like the aftermath of a break-in. What does it matter where he goes? He grabs only the cash, passport, checkbook, and Social Security card, and stuffs them in his pockets. He checks that the fridge is empty, that the burners are off. He shuts all the windows and locks them, turns all the lights on and off and on and off again.

He dials the airline and waits, holding the phone between his ear and shoulder, and locks the door behind him, imagining the apartment deteriorating over time, the windows turning brown, the floorboards warping, the air inside turning poison from stagnation. That's what standing still does. The only way to escape your own poison is to outrun it. He tugs on the doorknob one last time.

Get In

As she is pulling into the apartment complex, her phone rings, but it stops abruptly as she continues down into the underground garage and parks in her spot. As she is climbing the stairs, the phone beeps and she checks the message. She stops in the stairwell.

"Hi, hello," her boss says. "Listen, the office will be open again tomorrow, okay? I just have some things to take care of out of town, and then I'll come back. And you'll come back. I'll explain everything then, okay? Goodbye. Call me if you need anything. But, uh, I don't really know what you would need. All right then. Um…" he trails off, and the message ends with a beep.

Iris clicks the phone shut and continues up the stairs. She lets herself in, lets her things drop to the floor, and stands for a moment, staring at her apartment. She has never decorated per se, though she's lived here over two years. The walls look blank as the day she moved in. She feels now more than ever that she's simply been lodged here, another ice cube in a tray. She looks down at the dingy cream-colored carpet, and to the kitchen, the sink full of dirty dishes from single-girl dinners of ramen and crackers, the crumbs and sticky spots, and the hairs clinging to the furniture, the soap scum on the shower wall, all seem to encase her in an immobilizing dust. This is the mark she leaves. She thinks again of the ceiling fan at the bank, weighed down by grime, and swallows, the taste of her mouth stale, putrid. She then unbuttons her blouse, unzips her skirt, and lays these on the table.

She turns on the radio, and one of the Shangri-Las cries, "*Look out look out look out look out!*" followed by the sound of screeching tires and crunching metal. She twists her hair up in a knot and goes searching under the sink for bleach.

* * *

That night, sleep comes to her more easily than ever. She dreams that she is standing in front of the house, the family station wagon parked in the driveway. Her mother is filling the trunk with boxes. The roof is already strapped down with more belongings, camping gear, an old bicycle.

"Where are we going?" Iris asks.

Her mother's shoulders jump and she turns back to her, startled. "How long have you been standing there?"

Iris thinks, but can't remember not standing where she's standing. "I don't know. I think maybe a long time."

"Honey you have to pack your things, we're leaving tonight."

"But where are we going?"

"We're going. That's all you need to know right now."

"But why?"

Her mother doesn't answer as she pushes things around in the trunk, trying to make one last box fit.

Iris turns around to look at the houses across the street. The night is dark, and the windows are all lit, dotted with shadowy faces; the neighbors are watching.

She wanders out to the backyard, and as she gets close to the fig tree, she can hear a faint humming sound, and see the way the branches are moving with it. She looks up, and there, from one of the higher branches, she sees two small feet dangling, the rest of the body hidden by leaves.

She comes closer and a voice calls down, "Do you see me up here?"

"Yes," she says, "I see you."

"Do you dare me to jump?"

Iris tries to answer, but no sound comes out. She moves her lips soundlessly, over and over again, saying *no*, but not saying it.

She sees that the tree is buzzing with energy again, its edges blurred in vibration.

"Do you?" the boy says again, and Iris just stands there, watching the tree hum. The feet tuck back up under the leaves then, and Iris backs away.

When she gets back out to the driveway, the car is running and her father is in the driver's seat, her mother beside him.

He rolls down his window and yells out, "Neil!"

Iris looks and sees her brother standing in the middle of the road, far out ahead of them.

"Neil!" he yells again, to his son's back.

"Get in the car," her mother whispers to Iris without looking at her; she complies.

Her father switches on the headlights then, and Neil is illuminated, a towering figure far out in the distance. Iris squints, but can't tell if he is walking forward or standing still.

"We'll catch up to him," her mother says now, and her father nods to her and eases out of the driveway.

From the backseat, Iris looks back at the house, at the horses they are leaving behind, asleep on their feet, at the great tree shaking in the night, but she can't see the boy. She faces forward as the car rolls slowly down the road, Neil's figure still glowing up ahead, under the many watchful eyes, shielded behind glass.

* * *

Outside of Iris's sleeping body, her apartment sparkles whiter than white. She wiped down every surface with bleach-infused cleaners, their chemical scents masked with florals, vacuumed the carpet, washed the windows, mopped the kitchen floor, did all the dishes, hung all her clothes neatly in the closet, every-thing lined right up and stripped of germs, of dead skin cells and perspiration, of every trace of her body's occupation. She breathes it all in, this freshness, and this emptiness too.

And in the early morning, before she wakes, a new picture forms in her sleeping cells: a pine tree alone in a field, then suddenly, two trees, then three, multiplying faster than she can track until her consciousness is floating above a rapidly growing forest, new trees shoving themselves up out of the earth one by one, faster and faster, with a sound like a deck of cards, shuffling.

In One Room and Out...

Iris's alarm goes off at seven forty-five. She sits up quickly, the sheets suspended stiffly around her. She stares, grimacing at the clock, then suddenly realizes that the sound she's hearing isn't the beep of her alarm, but rather the sound of radio static, coming from inside her dresser.

She hops out of bed and pulls open the top drawer to find the little radio screaming its crackle and hiss and she presses the off button hard with her thumb. She checks the back and finds it loaded with batteries. She pats her hand around amid her socks and panties— no batteries there. She tries to remember taking them out. She can't remember. She sets the little radio down and rubs her eyes with her fists. Something is wrong here, but she can't remember.

She opens the bedroom window to let out the stuffiness, but it is stuffy outside too, another hot, stagnant day approaching. There is no airflow between inside and out. She pushes the screen aside and sticks her head out the window. It feels like just another room out there.

She turns on her radio to Motown Tuesday, which used to be Motown Monday, an arrangement that made a lot more sense, phonetically speaking. She gets in the shower just as "Heat Wave" is fading out, Martha Reeves wailing *yeah yeah, yeah ya-hah*, while the Vandellas sing quietly, *burnin', burnin', burnin'* just underneath. While she closes her eyes and lets the water pummel her face, the morning DJ comes on.

"That was a little Martha and the Vandellas— we all know something about heat waves around here, am I right? Well, it's only getting hotter, ladies and gentlemen. Our own meteorologist, Jenny "Sunshine" Samson tells me this is only the beginning. Stay inside with your head in the freezer today, kids, and don't come out until October! Jenny will join us with the full weather report in just a little while. Let's start our next block of Motown hits with a little more Martha— there's nowhere to run, kids, so stay right here!"

The bass and horns kick in, and Iris tries to separate Martha's song from the Vandellas'. This is what she always does with the girl groups. If she listens only to the background vocals, it's a different song. This one becomes more mournful, just the two voices in unison, repeating softly, *nowhere to run, nowhere to hide, ooooooohhh*. She opens up and lets the water fill her mouth. She swallows, though the water is considered poison here, provoking natives and transplants alike to fill their shopping carts with the bottled kind. It tastes all right to her. She turns the shower off and bends over in a quick jerking motion to wring out her hair; her jaw feels loosened from her skull.

She blow dries her hair and combs it smooth, puts on a dark green shift that zips up the back and has a straight neckline that makes her head and neck appear suspended above her body. It is a severe look that suits her today. Before she leaves the apartment, she stops at her dresser and picks up the little radio. It doesn't belong to her, she thinks, so she slips it into her bag, thinking it might be time she gave it back.

On the way into work, she stops for gas. She swipes her debit card, shielding her eyes from the already oppressive sun to make out the words on the screen. She enters her pin and waits, until the word "Declined" appears. Unsure if she's read it right, she brings her face in closer, cupping her hands between her temples and the edge of the screen. Her check hasn't cleared yet. She cancels the transaction and uses her credit card instead, a too-often-used standby whenever she's short. She tries not to think about what new heights her minimum payment due might reach next month.

When she pulls into the office parking lot, she is immediately struck by the number of cars, one next to another and another. She has to circle around to find a spot for the first time in as long as she can remember. She jerks the parking brake back too forcefully and turns the car off. She sits for a long minute, until it is too hot, before getting out, sliding sideways between her car and the black pickup truck next to it, parked on a diagonal, just over the line.

Inside and up the stairs, Iris sets her hand on the doorknob and fiddles with her keychain. She unwittingly turns the knob slightly while still isolating the office key, and the door opens, swinging slowly inward. She freezes. Her eyes dart to the lock, which doesn't appear to be broken. Still, her breath is caught in her throat. She gives the door the smallest push with her index finger, and it swings all the way to the wall and bounces lightly on the doorstop. She sets her left foot inside, then her right, one step at a time, the lavender carpet fibers bending under her weight. The lights are on, as she left them. She closes the door, sets her things beside her desk and sees her computer in screen saver mode, a red ball traveling slowly across the screen and bouncing lightly against each edge. She breaks up this serene tableau with a slide of the mouse and her desktop appears, adorned with the usual files and folders. The phone is where it is.

But there is something off. There is a new smell in the air, like metal, or smoke, a smell she can't decipher, if it is even there at all.

Then she shifts her gaze away from her desk and sees it on the wall in her own handwriting: *I will never be thirsty.* Words that were previously hidden behind the water cooler, the water cooler that is now gone, poof. Iris stands up straight, her vertebrae unlocking so she stands taller, her neck stretched like a bird's.

She goes up to the wall and runs her finger across the words, fixed like another coat of dried paint. She continues down the hall to the conference room. The round table and chairs are gone, the printer and fax machine too— just empty power outlets gaping their electricity.

She checks the storage room, flicking on the light and then flicking it quickly off again when she finds it bare. It's all gone.

She checks every room, one by one, turning slowly around and around, scanning the emptied spaces.

She buries herself deep in corners where desks, boxes, file cabinets, and electronics once sat.

She goes back to the empty storage room and runs her hands along each white wall. Then she stands back to examine the shared wall, and finds it smooth, top to bottom, end to end, until her eyes settle on her small spy hole. It gives her a moment of calm, seeing a second thing she has made that is still here.

But it doesn't last long, as she readies herself to open her boss's door. First, she checks all the other rooms again. There has to be something, she thinks. How many bits of paper shoved in drawers, fat file folders and coffee mugs, wastebaskets filled with empty ink cartridges and broken pencil lead, particleboard and wood, picture frames and plants and pens and confetti shaken from hole punches and stacks sky high of receipts and records and things that must be kept, referred to, filed away or not, things broken and things fixed, things forgotten and things used, picked over, touched, all the germs and dust and stray wires that poke, sharp things and dull things, and there has to be some trace, she thinks, if only in the air, something she could feel clinging to her skin. But the space grows more vacuous every time she looks, checks back one more time, tries her luck that something might appear this time, anything she might have overlooked— all the things, things, things that blocked her, that amounted to a ruin growing up around her, are just air now.

And there is one place left to look. She kicks the pumps off of her sweaty feet. Though the air conditioner still blasts, it feels so hot, and Iris is panting with exhaustion. She stands in front of her boss's closed door. She wraps her hand around the knob, taking care to remember everything that she's doing. She doesn't want to skip a crucial step.

Holding her breath, she turns the knob and steps inside. She lets her air out and stands slumped in the doorway. Her face betrays nothing. Her shock reserves must be tapped out, because she has no reaction to finding what she had to have known was waiting here.

She travels the perimeter of the office, scanning the walls for any sign of a trap door. Or anything. It doesn't have to be a clue, just an object, any one thing, because it is starting to feel so empty that she doesn't feel that she can ever leave. She will always be looking. She turns around and around, until she is dizzy, and the room seems to tip ever so slightly sideways. She thinks for a moment that maybe looking at it this way will do the trick, will tell her where to look. She finally stops when her legs wobble, threatening to pitch her down onto the floor.

She stumbles back out to the lobby, where her own desk sits untouched, business as usual. Then she notices that the phone on her desk, the phone that has barely rung in weeks, that anchors her desk, that is the main component of her job description— it's unplugged. The wire hangs slack off the end of the desk. She picks up the receiver out of habit and grips it in her hand, listens, but of course, there's only the sound of plastic pressed to her ear. But the motion gives her a moment of clarity. She finds the socket in the wall and when she gets a dial tone, punches in the speed dial code for her boss's cell. A second after she dials, a soft chiming tune sounds in her ear, followed by a soothing feminine alto, *I'm sorry, the number you have dialed is no longer in service. Please try again…*

She drops the receiver back on its cradle and, staring blankly forward, yanks the cord back out of the wall.

Iris could stand here, might stand here, forever, her arms at her sides and eyes bone dry. But eventually she swivels on her feet, steps in front of the desk and looks at it head on, as everyone who has ever passed her desk has seen it, as her boss saw it every day, or didn't see it, rushing past her hello to attend to whatever pressing business lay before him. It seems so low to the ground. She sinks then to her knees, crawls underneath it, and lays her head on a nest of wires, to collect her thoughts.

There is a panic that doesn't disrupt, but lives unnoticed in the body, that comes not as a shot from nowhere, but as a kind of liquid, released from within. As Iris lies beneath her desk, the only cover available, the panic, set loose from somewhere inside her, dormant for who knows how long, runs slowly, thickly through her veins. *My job*, she thinks, *My job*.

And on the underside of the desk, on the bare wood above her, unseen and forgotten by Iris in her fetal position, face pressed to the carpet: *Hello and good luck with the earthquake.*

But, she thinks, then. *But*— maybe no one knows she is here. Maybe no one has to know.

She reaches her arms out and slides forward, and as she emerges, half hidden beneath the desk and half splayed out under the fluorescent lights, she remembers that there is another place she has to look. She scrambles to her feet and rushes into the storage room.

Iris crouches down on the floor and lines up her right eye with the hole. She aims her gaze squarely toward the center of the room, and what she sees is… nothing. She is unable even to discern carpet or wall, or any texture at all— it's just a wash of emptiness, nothing, no color even, she can't even call it air. She blinks several more times, tries her left eye, wonders if she is losing her vision, and then she wonders if this is what she can expect to happen next. She will turn back to face her own office and find even the structure of the building gone, even the street, the whole landscape of the earth just a projection for which the unseen power source has been switched off. She would look down at her own body and find no body, she would look, and— there would be no she, no look.

While this series of events makes her blood pulse faster through her veins, causes her eyelids to flutter, she looks back from the hole and is relieved to find that she is still in a room. She stands again, her knees tattooed with carpet burn.

And then as she staggers back out in front of her desk, she hears noises coming from the hallway— footsteps, rustling fabric, clearing throats. She freezes, then edges slowly toward the door, which she opens very gently and pokes her head out of to find a line of people, waiting. Young and old, men and women, she eyes them one by one. They stand sixteen deep, reaching past the restrooms, almost into the shadows at the far end of the hall. The lineup starts at the door of suite 2B. She watches, waiting for any one of them to look up, but they are each thoroughly self-contained, consulting folders and notes, or arms crossed, waiting with beatific calm. At the front of the line, two feet in front of her at most, a young man stares at the closed door in front of him, straightening his tie. She doesn't think any of them notice her.

Then the door opens and before the man can step forward, Iris jumps ahead of him and steps inside, shutting the door quickly behind her. She stands with her back to it for a moment, taking in what she sees before her.

A red-headed woman in her twenties stands in front of a glass desk. She looks up at Iris, startled, and smiles.

"Hello, are you first?"

There's a knock on the door and Iris smiles tightly.

"I guess so," she replies, then looks around past the

receptionist's desk, struck by its layout, the virtually identical similarity to her own office.

"Um, first for…" Iris blurts out.

"You're here to interview, right?"

Still clinging to the door, both hands behind her back, wrapped around the doorknob, Iris asks, "How long have you been here?"

"I got in at eight-thirty?" she says, tilting her head in question.

"No, I mean, how… how long has this been here?" Iris is startled, as she suddenly feels her bare feet against the carpet and wonders if the woman has noticed.

"Um…" the woman looks around behind her, then turns back to Iris, "I don't know… I'm new. Shall I lead you back to the conference room for your interview?"

Iris nods slowly, and lets go of the door. She glances down at the wall on her right, where the other side of the hole ought to be, and only because she's looking for it, only because she knows where to look, she perceives the unevenness of fresh spackle.

She catches up to the woman, and follows as she leads her through another door, the door she couldn't open, and down a well-lit hallway. She lags behind again, trying to envision where this space has come from, where it fits into the building as a whole, but her spatial sense is failing her. She keeps picturing the side of the building bulging with add-ons. But there could always have been other doors she never noticed, opening to places she could never visit. Iris continues behind her down the hallway, which she now notes is just like her hallway, and the red-headed woman approaches the door, which is just like her boss's door, even the light is the same, the no smell in the air, the white of the walls, the lavender carpet, and in the moment it takes for the woman to get the door open, she is transported, and wonders if maybe she will work here now, or *does* work here now and maybe this is how these things are done.

When Iris reaches the open door, she finds the woman

leaning out the window, her hands gripping the sill. Then she pulls her head back inside and turns to face Iris, her face frozen in bewilderment.

"He was here just a minute ago."

"Who was?"

"My boss— he's supposed to be conducting staff interviews all day— we've got a line outside— I... he was just here."

Iris watches the woman's expression shift from confusion to annoyance.

"And... you think he could have gone out the window?"

The woman shakes her head and wraps a hand around her chin.

"No, no, that's ridiculous."

Iris steps to the window then and glances out over the street, at the glass storefronts and rushing cars. There doesn't seem to be anywhere to go.

"Well we're going to have to do this later. I don't know what to tell you." The woman leaves the room, slowly shaking her head.

After checking out the window once more, Iris backs calmly out of the office and closes the door behind her, coolly down the hall, trying to figure out what her next move ought to be. She passes the receptionist's desk, where the woman is staring at her computer screen, typing, with the telephone receiver clamped between her chin and shoulder. As she passes, Iris watches the woman, who could be her, who *is* her, essentially, and remembers the diner on the cliff, her place for so long and so long ago, and her fear that she would float up and off, and as she opens the door out into the hallway, she looks back at the receptionist, who for now remains a separate person, now scribbling something onto a notepad, and turns away quickly, for fear that she might find herself in the chair instead, with a fresh headache roiling.

Out in the hall, all eyes turn to her and she stumbles. She'd momentarily forgotten about them. She turns back to the receptionist, who looks up and mouths, "I'm sorry," before politely waving her off. Iris shuts the door behind her, clutching the knob on this side now, and clears her throat.

"There aren't going to be any interviews today, so you can all go," Iris announces, not making eye contact with anyone. She looks above them, to the side, around the edges of the crowd, and tries to slip quickly back through her own door. The man she cut in line grabs her bicep.

"I need this job," he says, imploringly, and Iris lets her arm go limp.

"I know," she says, still avoiding his eyes.

"I drove an hour to get here!" a woman near the back cries out.

The man grips her arm tighter and says, "Are you hiring?"

Iris looks into his wet, bloodshot eyes and the deep crows' feet around them and feels her resolve draining from her body, her head hollow and fuzzy, until finally, a surge of adrenaline kicks in. She wrenches her arm out of his grip, and thrusts herself into 2A, shutting and locking the door behind her, which doesn't stop people from knocking, or from turning and rattling the knob.

Iris abandons the door, breathing quickly, and returns to her boss's office. She could stay here, watch and wait. She still has a key, some claim on the space. Some tie to something. She looks out the window at the row of cars in the parking lot. She turns away from the window and tries to imagine what she will do if she stays, how long she might keep herself awake, and that's when her gaze settles on the rectangle in the carpet— the hatch, the trap door.

She drops to her knees and crawls over to it, lifting up the carpet flap to find the loose floorboard still loose. She pulls it up with her fingers and reaches down into the hole. She feels around, her palm hitting splintery beams of wood. She flattens herself on the carpet and reaches her head down into the hole, and is struck by the musty air, the mossy smell of old wood.

But she sees something. Beneath the knot of beams, the moldering guts of the building, there is a spot of light. Carefully, she leans in further, easing her shoulders through. She pauses, catching her breath, then reaches down lower, until she's waist-deep in the floor, and finds that she's able to pull herself deep into the interior, collecting soot and spider webs on her hands, in her hair, as she squeezes her body through this impromptu tunnel. She coughs, and a cloud of dust erupts before her eyes, now tearing. Finally, even her feet have disappeared inside the hole, and she balances herself like a gymnast, down the beams like a young monkey, and for a moment all is forgotten, there is only the physical challenge before her, and her focus is pulled by the light down below, growing, widening, as she slithers toward it, her limbs scraping against the jagged wood.

When the light is close enough for her to touch, she pushes further still, and finds that she's able to stick her hand right through. She stretches her wrist as far as it will stretch, wiggling her fingers, until they touch what feels like burning sand. The surrounding wood is so dank and decrepit that she manages to break apart a space just big enough for her to squeeze her body all the way through, the wood crumbling further as she wiggles her legs as though she were swimming.

She tumbles out onto the sand, sneezes, and rises up onto all fours, sticky grime between her fingers, her dress torn from hem to hip.

Once on her feet, Iris digs her bare toes into the sun-soaked dirt. The sky is bright, the dusty terrain endless, like the surface of another planet. Squinting against the harsh sunlight, the only thing Iris can make out is a tall ridge in the distance, red and claylike. Along the top of it, massive, precarious-looking rocks jut toward the sun, casting a shadow that looks serrated against the sand, like shattered glass spread on a windowsill. She begins walking toward it, as a slow breeze builds, blowing her footsteps clean away as soon as she's made them, so she leaves no mark, and in turn, nothing leaves a mark on her.

She keeps going, thinking briefly about the sunburn she must be incurring, but is she even outside? She looks up at the bleached sky, the close-up sun. It feels like sun, like air, and what can it be, if not only, exactly, what it feels like?

The longer she walks, the farther away the ridgeline seems, as though it's receding in space intentionally, to keep her away. Maybe she's just exhausted. The sky fades from white to a smoky tan as it bleeds into the earth. She is all alone out here, and remembers what her mother said to her when she was a girl, about walking alone, over a sink full of breakfast dishes:

Latch your focus onto something way off in the distance, like you're not even there, like you already walked by a long time ago.

No one can hurt you if you're not even there.

Iris swallows, and fixes her sights on the ridge, the only vertical entity on this horizontal plane, the jagged red against the bleached earth, remembering her mother's hands plunged in the sudsy sink, her fine-boned hands always raw, and her thin lipped profile, her expression shrouded by bug-like sunglasses on walks through that old neighborhood, through the gauntlet of wary eyes, the shaking heads, hovering by their front doors and kitchen windows, closed off by the steel of her mother's forward momentum. All at once, she misses her, and her father too, and Neil, *Oh god*, she thinks, what is it she wants to go back to? Not a place. It's a snapshot she longs for, the ability to remain inside a still image of a blue-sky summer morning, to hold a feeling, to never lose it down the well of time...

...And then she hears the delicate trill of a piano, the opening strains of a song so beautiful, so heart-stopping in its familiarity. It's coming from behind the ridge.

Iris takes off running, stirring up a breeze that dries her sweat, and the music swells louder, until she recognizes it, and is now running while singing barely audibly, somewhere in the back of her throat... *You-oooo send me, darling, you-oooo send me...*

She's so lost in her body's movement, in the music, in the sun burning through her skin, that she nearly runs right into the rock face, but veers left just in time to run alongside it, enclosed in its shadow like a magnet dragged across sheet metal, and when she turns the corner, there he is, playing, alone, cradled on all sides by low yellow dunes. Slowly, she comes up from behind, careful not to make any sound as she creeps around to face him, still whisper-singing, *honest you do, honest you do, honest you do...* though she doesn't know she's doing it.

The man from 2B stops playing when he sees her. He pulls his hands gently from the keys.

"Where are we?" she says.

"Underneath." He leans away from the keys and slumps down on the bench.

"Why didn't you tell me?" she says.

"You shouldn't be here," he says. He gets up off the bench and settles into a well-worn spot in the sand, leaning into one of the piano's legs.

Iris gets down on her knees beside him. The sand is hot at first, but the warmth it sends through her skin, the way it seems to massage her blood, is so soothing, she forgets the burn.

"There's nothing up there anymore," she says.

The man shakes his head.

"Let me stay."

"No," he shakes his head again, "you can't. It's not up to you, or me."

All the emotions stirred up by the morning's discovery converge, and an ache pulses in her breastbone, her eyes pleading.

"I'm here now," she says, her voice breaking. A tear rolls down her face, under her jaw, and settles in the hollow of her throat.

He looks up at her and smiles, then looks back to the ground.

"There's nothing to go back to," she whispers.

She watches his fingernails as they trace parallel lines in the yellow sand, the yellow sand tracing parallel lines under his fingernails, and feels all at once that they are made up of the same stuff, she, he, the dry earth beneath them, and the building falling to pieces above. She thinks to reach a hand out, to place it over his, but the act seems superfluous.

They sit together in silence for a moment, until it's broken by a loud buzzing followed by a twinkling chime. She instinctively pats her hands down her hips, but remembers her phone is back in the office. It's as loud as if it were right there on her person.

"You're going to want to get that," he says.

"But, I don't even..."

"You don't know who it could be."

They lock eyes, and Iris is overpowered by curiosity. It's true. It could be anyone calling, anyone at all. She rises back onto her feet.

"I'll be right back," she says. "Don't go anywhere."

She runs in the direction of the ringing, back the way she came, around the ridge and through the dust, with the sun pressing down, all the while imagining that she is on rails. She can do anything, and assume the rails have been well laid, and will lead her to wherever it is she needs to go.

She finds the hole she crawled out of to get here and finds the wood sagging. She has to push with all her strength to reopen the hole and squeeze her way back through, the buzzing, the ringing, filling her ears. She pushes up through the grime and slime as though through the guts of a sea monster, every beam, every bolt shifting and sliding. The building's interior is falling in on itself, melting almost, attaching itself to her flesh as she climbs up the barely holding rungs she just climbed down.

When she reaches the top, Iris heaves herself out onto the lavender carpet and sucks down air as she clamors for her purse. She punches her arm into its recesses and pulls out the phone, NEIL flashing on the screen.

"Hello?" she says, "Neil?"

She hears the beating of his heart, and behind it, a whirring of air.

"Neil, can you hear me?"

She hears a faint ding and a woman's voice, garbled as though coming through tiny speakers. A silence follows.

"Neil!" she yells. "Neil! It's me! Pick up, I'm here!"

"Hello?" he says, quietly, puzzled. "Iris?"

"Where are you?"

"I'm, oh, I guess I forgot to turn my phone off. We're about to take off. I've got to go…"

"Where are you going?"

"I'm just going away for a while."

"Where? Will you tell me, just once, where you're going?"

"Can you hear that?" he says abruptly.

"What is it?"

"That's the engine getting ready. Soon all you'll be able to hear is wind rushing behind it."

"Tell me where you're going and I won't tell anyone, I promise."

The fasten seatbelt sign lights up, and Neil's heart flutters in anticipation.

"You know that feeling? The mounting altitude? The thinning air? Your ears pop, and for once, you're inside your body completely? And it doesn't matter where you're going, because you're only going up?"

"Neil, please? I miss you. You know that, don't you? Tell me you know it?"

He doesn't answer. She hears the rushing rumbling, and then silence. He's gone.

Iris sinks back on her heels and tucks the phone back in her purse. Her hand lands on the little radio. This is what she came to do, to give it back, or to share it, if he'll let her. She slings the purse across her chest and crawls back to the hole. She wipes her sweating hands on the carpet in preparation to climb back through to the underneath, not thinking any further than that, feeling only that she needs the land and the sun, and to get away from these walls, when the walls themselves begin to quiver and quake.

She jerks her head up and sees the light fixtures shaking, and, forgetting all earthquake protocol, she dives her head and arms into the hole as planned, but it's too late. The beams she climbed down and up again have splintered and folded into each other like toothpicks, the space between them liquefied, collapsing in further with every shake of the frame.

She lurches up onto her knees, onto her feet, and runs for the front door to find it moving, a cacophony of garbled voices building just outside. She stands still for a moment, until the door is struck with a series of loud thumps and she flinches. Another smack and the door pops a hinge.

She panics, thinking there's nowhere to go, no way of escaping, and suddenly, with a great sucking sound, the walls drop several inches. She loses her balance, experiencing vertigo as the whole building sinks slowly, lopsidedly, toward the weeds around its perimeter and the burning tar smell of the parking lot fills her nostrils.

She scrambles back up onto her feet, and, not quite at her eye level, but not too far up, there is the window, the window she stared up at all that time, wondering what it was for, what it looked out on.

It's been waiting for this.

Her desk behind her has toppled into a heap, *kindling*, she thinks, as she hooks a foot up onto the aluminum windowsill and heaves herself up, so she is teetering on its edge. She gives the screen a strong push and watches it loosen and flap downward, landing with a scrape on the pavement.

It did look out. She could've had a view all this time, if only they'd put it just a little lower, where she could see. Would it have helped? Out there, everything looks the same as always. The pavement glittering just barely in the sun, the stores' window displays, sylph-like mannequins and brightly colored signs, traffic lights red, yellow, and green, the café where she had her lunch nearly every day, operating as usual. She thinks she can make out the two old men at their chessboard.

And there too is the vacant lot, and the sign that used to be.

I'm home. Are you?

I'm home. Where?

I'm home. So what?

Not there, but still there in her memory, and that counts for something. The window frame shakes and Iris holds on for balance and then realizes, there's no reason to hold on. *There's nothing up there anymore.*

It's not so far down, she thinks, and without even daring herself, without waiting another moment, she leaps, and for the seconds she's flying, she feels it too, the rush of air, the cloud wall filling her ears, the feeling that her body is her one and only home, and that that's as it should be, as it is and ever was.

She lands with a bone-loosening thud, but keeps going, her momentum too great to do anything but run, her bare soles picking up the city, taking her path with her as she goes.

Behind her, the building continues caving in on itself, but no one seems to notice. It sinks faster into the earth, sucked in as though the pavement were quicksand, gradually disappearing under the black tar of the parking lot into unknown earth, while people walk by on their way to appointments, meetings, and lunches. Soon, it will be just an empty space, to be filled or not, for the weeds to overgrow or wilt away.

As she runs, Iris clips the ear of a dog on a leash, startling his owner, who nearly drops the cup of coffee she's just bought. The woman collects herself and squints into the midday sun in an effort to figure out what's just happened, but Iris is long gone, the dog howling after her, into the wind. ∎

ACKNOWLEDGEMENT

I'd like to thank my parents, Bill and Mary Jetter, and my sister, Madeleine Jetter, for always providing a force of quiet yet unyielding support. I owe a tremendous amount to all the teachers who have helped me along the way, but most especially Bruce Bauman, for being such a consistent and dedicated mentor, Steve Erickson, for offering boundless inspiration, and to Aimee Bender and T.C. Boyle, for nurturing my initial desire to write and giving me the confidence to keep doing it. To the early readers, including Sara Finnerty and my other peers at CalArts, Blake Hennon, and Kim Samek, thank you for saving me from the vacuum. I am forever indebted to my wonderful agent, Judy Heiblum, and to Eric Obenauf and Eliza Wood-Obenauf, for being the best editors I could have hoped to work with. In no particular order, I must also express my gratitude to Kimby Caplan, Pete Larsen, Kelli McDonald, Heather Owen, Orli Low, CalArts and *Black Clock*. And finally, I could not have written this book without the love and encouragement of my husband, Abraham Kinney.

Also published by **TWO DOLLAR RADIO**

THE ORANGE EATS CREEPS
A NOVEL BY GRACE KRILANOVICH
A Trade Paperback Original; 978-0-9820151-8-6; $16 US
* National Book Foundation 2010 '5 Under 35' Selection.
* NPR Best Books of 2010.
* *The Believer* Book Award Finalist.

"Krilanovich's work will make you believe that new ways of storytelling are still emerging from the margins." —*NPR*

THE CORRESPONDENCE ARTIST
A NOVEL BY BARBARA BROWNING
A Trade Paperback Original; 978-0-9820151-9-3; $16 US

"A deft look at modern life that's both witty and devastating."
—*Nylon*

"Intelligent... a pleasure to read."
—*Bookslut*

THE CAVE MAN
A NOVEL BY XIAODA XIAO
A Trade Paperback Original; 978-0-9820151-3-1; $15.50 US
* *WOSU* (NPR member station) Favorite Book of 2009.
"As a parable of modern China, [*The Cave Man*] is chilling." — *Boston Globe*

THE VISITING SUIT
A NOVEL BY XIAODA XIAO
A Trade Paperback Original; 978-0-9820151-7-9; $16.50 US
"[Xiao] recount[s] his struggle in sometimes unexpectedly lovely detail. Against great odds, in the grimmest of settings, he manages to find good in the darkness."
—Lori Soderlind, *New York Times Book Review*

Also published by **TWO DOLLAR RADIO**

THE PEOPLE WHO WATCHED HER PASS BY
A NOVEL BY SCOTT BRADFIELD
A Trade Paperback Original; 978-0-9820151-5-5; $14.50 US

"Challenging [and] original… A billowy adventure of a
book. In a book that supplies few answers, Bradfield's lavish
eloquence is the presiding constant."
—*New York Times Book Review*

THE DROP EDGE OF YONDER
A NOVEL BY RUDOLPH WURLITZER
A Trade Paperback Original; 978-0-9763895-5-2; $15.00 US
* *Time Out New York*'s Best Book of 2008.
* *ForeWord* Magazine 2008 Gold Medal in Literary Fiction.
"A picaresque American *Book of the Dead*… in the tradition
of Thomas Pynchon, Joseph Heller, Kurt Vonnegut, and
Terry Southern." —*Los Angeles Times*

BABY GEISHA
STORIES BY TRINIE DALTON
A Trade Paperback Original; 978-0-9832471-0-4; $16 US

"[The stories] feel like brilliant sexual fairy tales on drugs.
Dalton writes of self-discovery and sex with a knowing
humility and humor."
—*Interview Magazine*

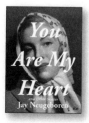

YOU ARE MY HEART AND OTHER STORIES
STORIES BY JAY NEUGEBOREN
A Trade Paperback Original; 978-0-9826848-8-7; $16 US

"[Neugeboren] might not be as famous as some of his
compeers, like Philip Roth or John Updike, but it's becoming
increasingly harder to argue that he's any less talented…
dazzlingly smart and deeply felt."
—Michael Schaub, *Kirkus Reviews*

Also published by **TWO DOLLAR RADIO**

SEVEN DAYS IN RIO
A NOVEL BY FRANCIS LEVY
A Trade Paperback Original; 978-0-9826848-7-0; $16.00 US

"The funniest American novel since Sam Lipsyte's *The Ask*."
—*Village Voice*

"Like an erotic version of Luis Bunuel's *The Discreet Charm of the Bourgeoisie*." —*The Cult*

DAMASCUS
A NOVEL BY JOSHUA MOHR
A Trade Paperback Original; 978-0-9826848-9-4; $16.00 US

"*Damascus* succeeds in conveying a big-hearted vision."
—*The Wall Street Journal*

"Nails the atmosphere of a San Francisco still breathing in the smoke that lingers from the days of Jim Jones and Dan White." —*New York Times Book Review*

TERMITE PARADE
A NOVEL BY JOSHUA MOHR
A Trade Paperback Original; 978-0-9820151-6-2; $16 US
* *Sacramento Bee* Best Read of 2010.

"[A] wry and unnerving story of bad love gone rotten. [Mohr] has a generous understanding of his characters, whom he describes with an intelligence and sensitivity that pulls you in. This is no small achievement." —*New York Times Book Review*

SOME THINGS THAT MEANT THE WORLD TO ME
A NOVEL BY JOSHUA MOHR
A Trade Paperback Original; 978-0-9820151-1-7; $15.50 US
* *O, The Oprah Magazine* '10 Terrific Reads of 2009.'

"Charles Bukowski fans will dig the grit in this seedy novel, a poetic rendering of postmodern San Francisco."
—*O, The Oprah Magazine*